Colette, the creator of Claudine, Chéri and Gigi, and one of France's outstanding writers, had a long, varied and active life. She was born in Burgundy in 1873, into a home overflowing with dogs, cats and children, and educated at the local village school. At the age of twenty she was brought to Paris by her first husband, the notorious Henry Gauthiers-Villars (Willy), writer and critic. By dint of locking her in her room, Willy forced Colette to write her first novels (the Claudine sequence), which he published under his name. They were an instant success. But their marriage (chronicled in *Mes Apprentissages*) was never happy and Colette left him in 1906. She spent the next six years on the stage – an experience, like that of her country childhood, which would provide many of the themes for her work. She remarried (*Julie de Carneilhan* 'is as close a reckoning with the elements of her second marriage as she ever allowed herself'), later divorcing her second husband, by whom she had a daughter. In 1935 she married Maurice Goudeket, with whom she lived until her death in 1954.

With the publication of *Chéri* (1920) Colette's place as one of France's prose masters was assured. Although she became increasingly crippled with arthritis, she never lost her intense preoccupation with everything around her. 'I cannot interest myself in anything that is not life,' she said; and, to a young writer, 'Look for a long time at what pleases you, and longer still at what pains you'. Her rich and supple prose, with its sensuous detail and sharp psychological insights, illustrates that personal philosophy.

Her writing runs to fifteen volumes: novels, portraits, essays, *chroniques* and a large body of autobiographical prose. She was the first woman President of the Académie Goncourt, and when she died was given a state funeral and buried in Père-Lachaise cemetery in Paris.

COLETTE

RIPENING SEED

TRANSLATED FROM THE FRENCH
Le Blé en Herbe
BY ROGER SENHOUSE

PENGUIN BOOKS
IN ASSOCIATION WITH
SECKER AND WARBURG

PENGUIN BOOKS

Published by the Penguin Group
27 Wrights Lane, London w8 5TZ, England
Viking Penguin Inc., 40 West 23rd Street, New York, New York 10010, USA
Penguin Books Australia Ltd, Ringwood, Victoria, Australia
Penguin Books Canada Ltd, 2801 John Street, Markham, Ontario, Canada L3R 1B4
Penguin Books (NZ) Ltd, 182–190 Wairau Road, Auckland 10, New Zealand

Penguin Books Ltd, Registered Offices: Harmondsworth, Middlesex, England

First published 1923
Published in Great Britain by Martin Secker & Warburg Ltd 1955
Published in Penguin Books 1959
7 9 10 8 6

This translation copyright © Secker & Warburg Ltd, 1955
All rights reserved

Printed and bound in Great Britain by
Cox & Wyman Ltd, Reading
Typeset in Bembo

Except in the United States of America,
this book is sold subject to the condition
that it shall not, by way of trade or otherwise,
be lent, re-sold, hired out, or otherwise circulated
without the publisher's prior consent in any form of
binding or cover other than that in which it is
published and without a similar condition
including this condition being imposed
on the subsequent purchaser

I

'ARE you going fishing, Vinca?'

With a haughty toss of her head, Vinca, the Periwinkle, with eyes the colour of April showers, replied that indeed she was going fishing. Her much-mended pullover and her sand-shoes hardened by brine showed that she was. Surely it was obvious that her blue-and-green-checked skirt, three years old and now well above her knees, belonged to shrimps and crabs. And did the two shrimping-nets across her shoulder, and her woollen beret, blue and thistly as the sea-holly on the dunes, denote any other rig than that for fishing?

She passed her questioner, and went on down towards the rocks with long strides of her well-shaped, slender legs, the colour of terra-cotta. Philippe watched her walking, comparing this year's Vinca with the Vinca of last year's holidays. Had she stopped growing yet? It was high time that she did! She had hardly filled out at all since a year ago. She had been letting her hair grow for the last four months, but it stuck out from her head like stiff corn-stalks glinting in the sun, and could not be plaited or curled. Her hands and cheeks were tanned almost black, but her neck under the hair was milk-white; her smile was reserved, her laugh spontaneous, and, though she was careful to fasten her blouses and jumpers over a non-existent bosom, she tucked up her skirt and knickers as high as she could when paddling with the unconcern of a small boy.

The companion who was watching her so intently lay stretched on a dune tufted with long wiry grass, his cleft chin resting on his crossed arms. Since Vinca had just turned fifteen and a half, he was sixteen and a half. All through their childhood they had been united: now adolescence was driving them apart. Already, the previous year, they were exchanging cutting remarks and sly punches: now, at any moment, silence would fall between them so heavily that they preferred a fit of the sulks to the effort of conversation. But Philippe, born hunter and gay deceiver, and cunning, cloaked his uncommunicativeness in mystery, and made a weapon of everything that embarrassed him. He would experiment with a few deprecatory gestures, throw out a 'What's the use? You wouldn't understand . . . ' while Vinca could only remain silent, tongue-tied, the victim of her desire to question and be answered, and fight against a precocious, overpowering instinct to give all; fight, too, against the fear that Philippe who was changing daily, and hourly gaining in strength, might sever the tenuous moorings that drew him back each year, from July to October, to the bushy copse that overhung the shore and the seaweed-bearded rocks. Already he had a disconcerting way of staring at Vinca without seeing her, as if she were transparent – fluid – negligible. . . .

Next year, perhaps, she will fall at his feet and use the speech of a grown-up woman: 'Phil, don't be unkind to me. . . . I love you, Phil. Do what you like with me. . . . Say something to me, Phil!' But for the present she still preserves the wayward dignity of a child and offers resistance – a resistance that Phil resents.

His eyes followed the boyish, graceful figure on its way down the slope to the sea. He had no more wish to kiss than to beat her, but he wanted her to trust in him and promise to be his alone, to do what he liked with as he could with the treasures he was ashamed of: pressed flowers, agate marbles, seeds and shells, picture-books, and a small silver watch.

'Wait for me, Vinca! I'm going fishing with you!'

She slowed down without turning round. He caught up with her in a few bounds and seized hold of one of the shrimping-nets.

'Why did you bring two?'

'I brought the small dip-net for the narrow holes, and my own because I always do.'

'So it wasn't for me, then?'

At the same time he held out a hand to help her across an awkward fissure in the rocks, and Vinca blushed beneath her tan. An unexpected look or gesture was sufficient to confuse her. Yesterday they had explored the cliff-face and climbed down the clefts side by side – each taking risks unassisted by the other. . . . Lithe and active as Phil, she could not remember having asked for his help.

'Steady on now, Vinca!' he protested with a smile as she snatched back her hand too sharply. 'What have I done to upset you now?'

She bit a lip cracked by the daily plunge and continued to pick her way over rocks that bristled with barnacles. The more she thought, the less certain of herself did she feel. What was he up to, in any case? Here he was, being charming and gallant, offering her his hand as he might to a lady. . . . Slowly she lowered the dip-net into a cavity where under the placid sea water she could clearly make out the various seaweeds, sea-cucumbers, blennies, wrasse, the father-lashers all head and fin, black-shell crabs etched with red, and shrimps. . . . Phil's shadow fell across the sunlit pool.

'Do get out of my light! You've gone and cast your shadow right over the shrimps and, what's more, this is my own special hole.'

He moved away, and she fished by herself, impatiently, with less than her accustomed skill. Ten, twenty shrimps eluded the too precipitate dab with her net and darted away to ensconce themselves in crannies, where they tested the water with their delicate whiskers and defied capture.

'Phil! Do come here, Phil! This place is alive with shrimps, and they simply won't let themselves be caught.'

He came back without much enthusiasm and leaned over the teeming little abyss.

'Of course they won't. You see, you don't know how. . . . '

'I know perfectly well how,' Vinca interrupted shrilly. 'I just haven't the patience, that's all.'

Phil sank the shrimping-net down to the bottom and kept it there motionless.

'In the crevice of that rock,' Vinca whispered over his shoulder, 'beauties, such beauties. Don't you see their little horns?'

'No. That doesn't matter. They'll soon come along out.'

'Do you really think so?'

She leaned further over and her hair, like the clipped wing of a captive bird, fluttered against her companion's cheek. She drew back, then involuntarily she came forward again, only to draw back once more. He seemed not to notice, but with his free hand he caught hold of her bare arm, tanned by sun and brine. 'Look, Vinca! Here comes the belle of the ball!'

Vinca stealthily withdrew her arm and it slipped as far as the wrist through Phil's hand as through a bracelet, for he did not tighten his grip. 'You'll never catch her, Phil. She's darted off again.'

So as to watch the shrimp's antics better, Vinca let her arm slide back right up to the elbow through his half-closed hand again. In the green water the long agate-grey shrimp was frisking on the ring of the net, testing it now with its legs, now with its feelers. One turn of the wrist and . . . But the fisherman delayed, perhaps enjoying the stillness of the unresisting arm under his hand and the weight of a head veiled in hair against his shoulder, a head that leaned submissive for a moment and then was jerked shyly away. . . .

'Quick, Phil, quick, pull up the net! . . . Oh, she's got away! Why did you let her go?'

Phil drew in his breath, and gave his young friend a look in which pride, tinged with astonishment, seemed to make light of his triumph. He let go the arm that seemed in no hurry to be freed, saying, as he stirred up the whole limpid pool with great sweeps of the shrimping-net, 'Oh, she'll come back. . . . It's just a question of waiting. . . .'

2

THEY were swimming side by side, his head round and black under his wet hair and his skin the whiter, hers the light gold that fair skins turn, a blue foulard round her head. The daily bathe, joy silent and complete, returned them to the peace and childhood they were in danger of losing at their difficult age. Vinca floated on her back, blowing water in the air like a young seal. Beneath the twisted foulard peeped two delicate pink ears, hidden by her hair during the day, and, on either temple, two clearings of white skin that saw the light only at bathing time. She smiled at Philippe, and under the eleven o'clock sun the delicious blue of her eyes took on a greenish reflection from the sea. All of a sudden he dived down, seized hold of one of her feet, and dragged her under the water. They 'drank a draught' together, and came to the surface again spitting, spluttering, and laughing, as though forgetful of their age, she of her fifteen years of tortuous love for her childhood companion, he of his sixteen years of domination, his debonair disdain, and the unreasonableness of his precocious sense of proprietorship.

'Race you to the rocks!' he shouted, striking for the shore.

But Vinca did not follow his lead, landing instead on the nearby sand.

'Are you getting out already?'

She tore off her cap as if she were scalping herself and shook out her stiff fair hair. 'There's a gentleman coming to lunch. Papa said I must dress for it.' Still wet, she started to run, tall and tomboyish but gracefully made, the muscles in her long legs hardly apparent. She drew up sharp at a word from Phil.

'Are you going to doll yourself up then? What about me? Can't I eat in a loose shirt in that case?'

'Of course you can, Phil. Anything you like. Besides, you look so much nicer in an open collar.'

The periwinkle eyes, set in a small dripping sun-burnt mask, suddenly expressed anxiety, a whim-of-the-moment desire for approval. Phil relapsed into haughty silence, and Vinca went on her way up the links starred with mauve scabious.

Left alone Phil muttered to himself as he churned up the water. Vinca's preferences meant little to him. 'I always look good to her . . . but this year she's never satisfied with anything.'

The apparent contradiction in these two sallies brought a smile to his lips. He turned turtle, and following her example floated on his back, letting the salt water fill his ears with rumbling silence. . . . Was it a wisp of cloud between him and the sun at its zenith? Phil opened his eyes to catch a glimpse overhead of the dun breast feathers – the dark legs forced back in flight – and the long tapering beaks of a pair of curlew.

'Of all the crazy ideas!' Philippe said to himself, 'No, it can't be true! What's come over her? She looks like an organ-grinder's monkey. She looks like a mulatto girl decked out in her Sunday best.'

Next to Vinca, and closely resembling her, her younger sister sat staring in front of her; she had china-blue eyes in a round sunburnt face under a thatch of wiry fair hair, and was resting her small fists on either side of her plate, like a well brought up child. Big and little sister alike were dressed in starched and ironed frocks of white flounced organdie.

'Sunday in Tahiti!' scoffed Philippe inwardly. 'I've never seen her look such a fright.'

Vinca's mother, Vinca's father, Vinca's aunt, Phil and his relations, and the visitor from Paris made a fringe round the table of green jumpers, striped blazers, tussore jackets. The villa, rented each year by the two families of friends, smelt this morning of hot brioches and bees-wax. The grey-haired Parisian stood out from among the sun-tanned children and multi-cloured bathers as a stranger, delicate, pale, and over-dressed.

'How quickly you change, little Vinca!' he said to the little miss.

'Don't I know it!' Philippe muttered peevishly.

The stranger leaned towards Vinca's mother, to whisper confidentially, 'She's going to be enchanting, really ravishing. Mark my words, in another two years ...'

Vinca overheard this remark, favoured him with a swift, utterly feminine glance, and smiled. Her wine-red lips parted on a strip of pearly teeth, her fair lashes fluttered over eyes as blue as her name-flower, and even Philippe himself was dazzled. 'What's this? What's she up to now?'

Vinca served the coffee in the linen-panelled hall. She executed this intricate manoeuvre deftly, with the accomplished poise of an acrobat. When a sudden gust threatened to overturn the flimsy table, she prevented a chair from toppling with her foot and with her chin a lace napkin from flying away, while at the same time she never stopped pouring an impeccable flow of coffee into one or other of the cups.

'Just look at her!' The stranger was in ecstasies, as he expatiated on her 'tanagra' figure, insisted that she sip a chartreuse, and asked her the names of all the young men whose hearts she had broken at the Cancale Casino.

'That's a good one, the Cancale Casino! There is no casino at Cancale.'

She laughed, showing the full range of her solid teeth, and spun round on the toes of her white shoes like a ballet-dancer. With coquettishness came guile: never once did she look toward Philippe, who, a sullen figure lurking behind the piano and the large copper jug filled with sea-holly, was watching her every move. 'I must be wrong about her,' he confessed to himself. 'She's really very pretty. She's got me guessing this time all right.'

When, at the sound of the gramophone, the stranger asked her to teach him the latest dance-steps, Philippe slipped out of doors, ran towards the beach and rolled himself into a ball in one of the sandy hollows, before letting his head rest on his arms and his arms on his knees. Behind his closed eyelids persisted the vision of this new Vinca, full of insolent allurement: a coquettish Vinca, quite suddenly endowed with rounded flesh and conscious of her charms; or a naughty, rebellious Vinca, according to choice.

'Phil, dear Phil, I've been looking for you everywhere. What's the matter?'

The enchantress was close beside him, panting, and tugging ingenuously at his forelock to make him look up.

'Nothing's wrong,' he answered in a husky voice.

He opened his eyes fearfully, to find her on her knees in the sand, ruining the ten flounces of her organdie dress and crawling before him like a squaw.

'Please, please, Phil, don't be cross! Have I done something to annoy you? Phil, you know I love you best in the world. Do say something to me, Phil!'

He searched everywhere for a trace of the momentary splendour that had provoked him. All he could see was a dismayed Vinca, a girl not yet fully mature, beset beyond her years by the awkwardness, the self-abasement, the forlorn persistence of someone really in love. He snatched away the hand she was kissing. 'Leave me alone can't you!

13

You don't understand . . . you never understand anything! And do get up off the ground!'

And he sought, as he smoothed the crumpled folds, tied the sash, patted into place the stiff hairs all on end in the wind, he sought to change her back into the little goddess who, for a moment, had flashed before his eyes.

3

'WE'VE just another month and a half of the holidays left, haven't we?'

'Only a month,' Vinca said. 'You know well enough I have to be in Paris by the twentieth of September.'

'Why? Your father's always had leave till the first of October in other years.'

'I know, but Mummy and I, and Lisette, haven't so very much time, between the twentieth of September and the fourth of October, for all our autumn business. My new party dress – and a coat. A hat for me – same for Lisette. . . . I mean to say, you know, we women . . . '

Phil was lying on his back, chucking fistfuls of sand in the air.

'Oh rot! You women, indeed! You make far too much fuss over all that.'

'We have to. . . . You, of course, find all your clothes laid out for you on the bed. All you worry about are your shoes, because you will buy them at a shop where your father forbids you to go. Apart from that, it's all plain sailing. Things are made so easy for you men. . . . '

Philippe sat bolt upright, ready to respond to her irony. But Vinca was not in joking mood. She was sewing, whipping a pink scallop on to a light linen frock that matched the colour of her eyes. Her fair hair, cut Joan-of-Arc style, was gradually growing longer. Sometimes she parted it at the back, tying it in two short whisks against her cheeks. She had lost one of her ribbons since lunch, and over that half of her face the hair flapped like a drawn curtain.

Philippe frowned. 'Lord, what a mess your hair's in, Vinca!'

She blushed under her holiday tan and a humble appeal crept into her eyes as she pushed back the hair behind her ear.

'I know it is. . . . It's bound to look untidy while it's kept so short. It's only trimmed this way, while waiting . . .'

'And you don't mind looking ugly in the meantime?' he asked harshly.

'I mind very much, Phil, I promise you I do.'

He was shamed into silence by her quiet acquiescence, and she looked up at him in astonishment, for she expected no mercy. He believed in a short-lived truce once he had hurt her feelings, and made ready for the next insult, the next childish sarcasm, for what he called the 'whippet-snaps' of his young friend. But she was smiling, a wistful, melancholy smile, addressed to the smooth sea and to the sky, where the high wind was drawing fern-patterns among the clouds.

'Whatever you may think, I really do want to look pretty, I promise you. Mummy says there's still a chance I may, but that I must have patience.'

At fifteen, she had the pride and gawkiness of her age, but those years had given her a body trained for running and walking, conditioned to all weathers, lean, firm, and hardened, at times not unlike a riding-switch that cuts and slashes; but the startling blue of her eyes and the clear simple line of her mouth were already the perfected traits of feminine beauty.

'Patience, indeed!' Phil leapt to his feet and with the toe of his shoe began scraping at the dry sand of the dune, pearly with little empty snail-shells. A hated word had just poisoned his siesta, the siesta of a schoolboy enjoying his holidays. In the full vigour of his seventeenth year, he could adapt himself to idleness and relaxation, but the idea of passive evolution, of having to wait patiently for developments, exasperated him. He clenched his fists, expanded his bare chest, and hurled defiance at the heavens.

'Patience! Good God! that's the one word you all of you have on the tip of your tongue! You, and my father, and my "beaks".'

Vinca dropped her sewing to stare in admiration at the harmonious figure of her companion, whose proportions lost nothing by his gangling age. Dark, white-skinned, and of medium height, he had been slow in growing and since fourteen had resembled a small, well-knit man, each year on a slightly larger scale.

'What else can we do, Phil? We have no choice. You seem to think if you stretch out your arms and swear to heaven you can bring about some change or other. You're not more wicked than the rest. You'll sit for your matric, and if you're lucky you'll get through.'

'Shut up! You talk like my mother.'

'And you like a child! What d'you hope to gain, my poor boy, by being so impatient?'

Philippe's dark eyes glared hatred at her because she had called him 'my poor boy'.

'I hope for nothing,' he said tragically. 'I don't even hope that you'll understand me. There you sit, with your pink scallop, babbling about going home, about your party dresses, and all that petty routine. Why, when I think that soon I'll be sixteen and a half . . . '

The periwinkle eyes, sparkling on the verge of tears, contrived to smile. 'Oh, yes! Just because you're sixteen you consider yourself master of the whole world! Is that what the films have done for you?'

To prove his mastery, Phil seized her by the shoulder and shook her.

'Didn't I tell you to shut up! Every time you open your mouth you let out something fatuous. . . . I'm fit to burst, to burst, I tell you, when I think I'm only sixteen! All the years ahead – years of exams, matric, professional training, years of messing about and groping in the dark – having to begin all over again if you fail, or be crammed with the stuff you couldn't digest properly the first time and so were ploughed. When you have to pretend to your people that you're dead keen on a career, so as not to distress them, while all the time you can see what desperate efforts they're making to appear infallible, though they know even less about you than you know yourself. Oh, how I detest this moment in my life, Vinca! Why can't I, all at once, be twenty-five!'

He radiated intolerance and a sort of traditional despair. In his haste to grow up and his contempt for the period when body and soul are like buds ready to burst into flower, this scion of a small Parisian industrial house was transformed into a hero of romance. He flung himself down at Vinca's feet and continued his lamentations. 'So many more years, Vinca, of being almost a man, almost free, almost in love.'

She put her hand on the raven locks tousled by the wind and now on a level with her knees, but she voiced none of the thoughts roused in her by an instinctive feminine wisdom. 'Only almost in love? Isn't it possible, then, to be no more than almost in love?'

Phil rounded on her violently. 'And what about you? You who put up with all that sort of thing, what do you propose doing?'

Under his dark glance her features again took on a look of uncertainty.

'The same as you, Phil. Only I'm not going to try to matriculate.'

'Then what are you going to do? Are you going in for industrial designing, or what? Or is it to be chemistry?'

'Mummy says . . . '

He kicked out in anger like a colt, though without standing on his feet.

'Mummy says, Mummy says! What a slavish little beast you are! And what does Mummy say?'

'She says,' Vinca repeated the words submissively, 'that she suffers from rheumatism, that Lisette is only eight, that there's plenty of work for me to do at home without my looking further afield, that soon I shall have to begin looking after the household accounts, help with Lisette's education, keep an eye on the maids, and all that sort of thing.'

'All that sort of thing! Less than nothing, in fact!'

'She says that I shall get married . . . ' She blushed and removed her hand from Philippe's head, seeming to hope for a word from him which never came. 'And finally, that until I do get married, there's plenty I can be getting on with.'

He turned round again and scanned her contemptuously.

'And that's enough for you, isn't it? That's enough for you for . . . let's see . . . for five or six years, perhaps more?'

Her blue eyes wavered but held his. 'Yes, Phil, while waiting. . . . Since we're only sixteen and fifteen, you and I. . . . Since we're forced to wait. . . . '

The shock of this detestable word shook his defences. Once again he was reduced to silence by the simplicity of his young friend, by the submissiveness she dared to put into words, by her way of paying homage, as a female, to trusty household gods, and, though disappointed by this, he felt vaguely appeased. Would he have welcomed a high-spirited Vinca, scenting adventure and pawing the ground, like a bridled filly, at the prospect of the long hard road through adolescence?

He pillowed his head against the dress of his childhood playmate. He felt her thin knees quiver, then press closer together, and with the sudden enthusiasm of youth, Philippe conjured up the vision of their delicate contours. But he closed his eyes, confiding the weight of his head to her safe keeping, and stayed like that, while waiting. . . .

4

PHILIPPE was the first to reach the road – two ruts in the dry shifting-sand, mobile as a wave, with a median ridge of sparse salt-bitten grass – down which the carts went to gather sea-wrack after the neap tides. He was resting against the two poles of the shrimping-nets and carried a couple of creels slung over his shoulder, having left Vinca to carry the two slender gaffs baited with raw fish, and his fishing blazer – a precious relic, with amputated sleeves. He treated himself to a well-earned rest and condescended to wait for his fanatical little friend, whom he had abandoned in the desert of rocks and pools and seaweed left uncovered by the August high tide. He tried to pick her out far below before he let himself slide down the bed of the road. Beyond the sandy declivity, among the scintillating sparks set off by the sun's rays striking a hundred little mirrors of water, a blue woollen beret, faded to the tint of sea-holly, marked the spot where Vinca was still hunting determinedly for shrimps and edible crabs.

'Ah, well, if it amuses her!' he said under his breath.

Then he let himself go, his bare back extracting a delicious thrill from contact with the fresh sand as he slid along the track. Close to his ear he could hear, issuing from the creels, the moist susurrus of a fistful of shrimps and the sharp scraping of a large crab's claw against the lid.

Phil sighed, overcome by a sense of vague unclouded happiness, in which his agreeable fatigue, the twitch of muscles still tensed after rock-climbing, and the warmth and colour of a Breton afternoon suffused with vaporized saline, each severally played its part. He sat down, dazzled from staring at the milky sky, and was surprised to see the new bronze texture of his arms and legs – the arms and legs of a sixteen-year-old – slender, yet fully moulded over taut, unobtrusive muscles, which could equally have been the pride of a girl in her teens as of a growing boy. He had grazed his ankle and it was bleeding. After wiping the abrasion with his hand, he licked his fingers and tasted the mingled saltiness of blood and brine.

An off-shore breeze wafted the scent of the new-mown after-crop, farmyard smells, and the fragrance of bruised mint: little by little, along the level of the sea, a dusty pink was usurping the domain of blue unchallenged since the early morning. Philippe did not know how to express such a thought as: 'All too few are the occasions in life when, with mind content, eyes surfeited with beauty, heart light, retentive, and almost empty, there comes a moment for the senses to be filled to overflowing: I shall remember this as just such a moment.' Yet the bleat of a goat and the tinkle of the cracked bell round its neck were enough to make the corners of his mouth quiver with anguish and his eyes fill with tears of pleasure. He did not let his eyes linger on the dripping rocks where Vinca was roaming, did not even breathe her name when experiencing his pure emotion: at the crisis of such unheralded delights, a child of sixteen would not know how to call for succour to another child, herself perhaps in a similar predicament. . . .

'Hi, there, young fellow-me-lad!'

The voice that woke him from his day-dream was young, authoritative. Phil turned toward it without getting up, to find a lady dressed all in white who, not ten yards from him, was digging the point of her walking-stick and the high heels of her white shoes into the sandy cart-track.

'Tell me, young fellow, there's surely no sense in trying to drive my car any further down this way, is there?'

Politeness made Philippe rise to his feet and go closer; but only when he was upright and could feel on his bare body the touch of the cool breeze, and the eyes of the lady in white, did he blush. She smiled and changed her mode of approach. 'Forgive me, monsieur . . . I was certain my chauffeur had made a mistake. I'd far better have sacked him on the spot. Surely this road ends up in a path that leads only to the sea?'

'Yes, madame. It's the sea-wrack road.'

'Cirac? And how far away is Cirac?'

Phil could not retain a burst of laughter, which the white lady obligingly echoed.

'Did I say something funny? Take good care, or I shall be calling you "young fellow" again. Now that you're laughing, you look no more than twelve.'

But she was looking him in the eyes, like a man.

'Madame, it's the sea-wrack track, not Cirac. . . . It's . . . it's used for the sea-wrack.'

'Most illuminating,' said the white lady, 'and I am much obliged to you for the explanation.'

She was pulling his leg as a man might, and her bantering tone corresponded to the frank way she was gazing at him, so that Philippe felt suddenly tired, feeble, and limp, overcome by an access of femininity that can paralyse an adolescent in front of a woman.

'Have you had a good catch, monsieur?'

'No, madame, nothing to speak of. . . . That's to say . . . Vinca caught more shrimps than I did.'

'And who is Vinca? Your sister?'

'No, madame, she's a friend of mine.'

'Vinca. . . . A foreign name?'

'No. . . . That's to say . . . It's short for Periwinkle.'

'Is she a girl of your own age?'

'She's fifteen. I am sixteen.'

'Sixteen . . . ' the white lady repeated after him.

She made no comment, but added a moment later, 'You've got sand on your cheek.'

He rubbed his cheek so violently that he almost drew blood, and then his arm fell back to his side. 'I've got no feeling in my arms,' he thought, 'I believe I'm going to be ill.'

The white lady relieved Phil of her tranquil gaze, and smiled.

'Here comes Vinca,' she said, indicating the corner of the road round which the figure of a girl had just appeared. She was lugging a wooden tackle-box, and Philippe's blazer. 'Good-bye, monsieur . . . ?'

'Phil,' he answered automatically.

She did not hold out her hand, but nodded her head two or three times like a woman replying 'Yes, yes,' to her own hidden thoughts. She was not yet out of sight when Vinca ran up.

'Phil, who in the world was that woman?'

A shrug of the shoulders, and a blank look on every feature, expressed his complete ignorance.

'You don't know her, and yet you were speaking to her?'

In answer Phil gave her a scathing glance, inspired by a return of his old malice, and shook himself free of his momentary yoke. He was joyfully aware of their respective ages, of the rift in their friendship already perceptible, of his own despotic behaviour and Vinca's sometimes petulant devotion. Still dripping wet, her scarred knees were worthy of a Saint Sebastian and perfect under their ravaged surface: her hands would have done credit to a garden-help or cabin-boy; a greenish handkerchief was knotted round her throat and her jersey carried the whiff of live mussels. The blue of her shaggy beret no longer vied with the blue of her eyes and, except for her anxious, jealous, eloquent eye, she might well have been a student dressed for a college rag. Phil began to laugh, and Vinca stamped her foot as she threw his blazer at him.

'Will you answer me, or won't you?'

As if not deigning to reply, he thrust his bare arms through the open arm-holes of his jacket.

'Don't be so stupid! It was just a lady with a car who had lost her way. A little further, and the wheels would have sunk in the sand. I redirected her.'

'Oh!'

Vinca had sat down and a shower of wet pebbles was pouring from her sand-shoes.

'And why did she go off in such a hurry just as I came into view?'

Philippe took his time before answering. Once more he savoured in secret the gestureless assurance, the frank gaze, and the thoughtful smile of the unknown lady. He recollected how serious she had been in calling him 'Monsieur'. But he also remembered how she had said 'Vinca' in a familiar, if not derogatory way. He knitted his brows, permitting a protective look to cover the innocent disorder of his little friend. He thought a moment longer before he hit upon an ambiguous answer that satisfied both his secret taste for romance and his middle-class prudery.

'As things turned out, she didn't do so badly,' was his answer.

5

HE tried entreaty. 'Vinca, look at me! Give me your hand.
... Let's think about something else.'

She turned away to the window and gently took her hand
from his.

'Leave me alone. I'm miserable.'

All that could be seen through the window was the
westerly weather of August, bringing rain in its wake. The
earth came to an abrupt end out there, on the brink of the
links. One more squall, one more upheaval of the great grey
field furrowed with parallel ridges of foam, and the house
must surely float away like the ark. ... But Phil and Vinca
knew the August seas of old and their monotonous thunder,
as well as the September seas and their crested white horses.
They knew that this corner of a sandy field would remain
impassable, and all through their childhood they had scoffed
at the frothy foam-scuds that danced powerlessly up to the
fretted edge of man's dominion.

For the second time Phil opened the french window,
closing it behind him with an effort; he put his head down
against the wind, and felt on his forehead the fine rain win-
nowed by the storm, the gentle drizzle, a little salty from
the sea, that travelled through the air like drifting smoke.
He started collecting the steel-weighted bowls and the box-
wood jack they had left out on the terrace that morning, and
picked up the tambourine-shaped racquets and the small
rubber balls. These playthings that no longer amused him he
stowed away in the shed, as one packs away the various bits
and pieces of a disguise that may come in handy again one
day. The periwinkle eyes followed his movements from

behind the closed window, and the raindrops trickling down the panes seemed to be streaming from her eyes, troubled now, but of a blue unaffected by the variegated dull pewter of the heavens or the leaden green of the waves.

Phil folded up the wooden chairs and tipped the bamboo table on its side. He did not smile at his friend as he passed. Gone were the days when they had need to smile to make each other happy, and there was nothing about the present day to bring them joy.

'Only a few more days, less than three weeks,' Phil said to himself, as he wiped the sand off his fingers on a moist tuft of wild thyme covered with flowers and tiny wood-wasps, caught in the rain and waiting for the first ray of sunshine. He breathed in the pure fresh fragrance on the palms of his hands, and resolutely resisted a wave of enfeebling nostalgia that threatened to bring back the melancholy of his seventh year. Instead, he looked up at the window, where, between the streaming tears of the rain and the twisted corollas of the moribund morning-glories, he could see on Vinca's face the grown-up expression she reserved for his eyes only and hid from all others behind the mask of a gay and sensible girl of fifteen.

A lull in the storm held the rain imprisoned in the clouds, and opened up a livid wound above the horizon, from which radiated an inverted fan of wan and dismal rays. Phil's heart leapt up when he beheld this omen in the sky, so eager was he to reap the just rewards and benefits to which his sixteen tormented years entitled him. Yet, though facing the sea, he was still aware of the closed window behind him with Vinca pressed against the panes. 'Only a few days more,' he repeated to himself, 'and then we'll be parted. What's to be done about it?'

It never crossed his mind that he had felt miserable and unhappy at the end of last year's holidays, until he returned to Paris and his day-school curriculum and became resigned to the consolations of Sunday. Last year Philippe had been fifteen: as each succeeding year came round, all that was not wrapped up with Vinca and himself he relegated to a dim and miserable past. Did he really love her as much as all that? he asked himself; and finding no other word but 'love' in answer, he furiously tossed back the hair from his forehead. 'Perhaps I don't really love her as much as all that, but the truth is she belongs to me. And that's all there is to it.'

He turned round toward the house and shouted into the wind, 'Come on out, Vinca! It's stopped raining.'

She opened the french window and stood there on the threshold like a convalescent, one shoulder hunched up to her ear, as if afraid.

'Do come on! The tide's on the turn and that means more rain.'

She tied a white foulard round her head, knotting it at the back, so that it looked like a bandage.

'Come on down as far as the Point, at least. It'll be dry there under the rock.'

She followed him without a word along the coast guard's path, cut in the cliff-face above the edge of the sea. They trod on pepper-scented marjoram and the last flowers of sweet clover. Below them the sea smacked like the flapping of torn flags and unctuously licked the foot of the rocks. Above them, near the top of the cliffs, its force drove back the warm gusts that wafted the odours of shell-fish and the earthly smell of the little ledges where seeds, sown by the wind and birds in flight, throve on a scrappy sustenance.

They reached their retreat, an eyrie unprotected on three sides, dry, and well sheltered under its prow of overhanging rock, where one had the illusion of heading straight for the open sea. Philippe sat down close beside Vinca, and she let her head sink against his shoulder. She had all the appearance of being utterly exhausted, and closed her eyes at once. Her fresh round rosy cheeks, sunburnt as they were and powdered with freckles, with something vegetal about the softness of their velvety down, had lost much of their colour since the morning; so had her ripe lips, which always looked crinkled, like fruit scorched by the heat of the day.

After lunch, Vinca, who usually cut short the jeremiads of her 'childhood sweetheart' by interposing with the stubborn, gentle, sound, common sense of an intelligent little bourgeoise, had burst into tears, into protestations of despair and bitter recriminations. She had inveighed against everything that at their tender age they found so hateful – the future that looked so unattainable, the impossibility of running away, and a resignation they could not bring themselves to accept. She had shouted 'I love you!' as some shout 'Good-bye!', and 'I can't ever bear to leave you!' with a look of horror in her eyes. Their love, which had grown up with them, had cast a spell over their childhood and protected their adolescence from vicarious friendships. Less ignorant than Daphnis, Phil had always treated Vinca as a brother, sometimes with respect, sometimes with roughness, but always with fondest affection, as though, after the manner of orientals, he and she had been married from the cradle. . . .

Vinca sighed, and opened her eyes again without raising her head.

'I'm not tiring you, am I, Phil?'

He shook his head, and gazed with admiration into her eyes, whose blue, each time more dear to his heart, flickered elusive between their fair-tipped lashes.

'Look out there,' he said. 'The storm is already dying down. There'll be another huge tide at four in the morning. . . . But we can trust that rift and expect a lovely full moonrise to-night.'

Instinctively he spoke of smooth seas and halcyon skies, to guide her thoughts toward serener images. But she gave no sign of response.

'You're coming to play tennis at the Jallons' to-morrow?'

She shut her eyes again and shook her head in sudden fury, as though refusing to eat or drink, or even to go on living.

'Vinca, you must!' Philippe was stern in his insistence. 'We'll have to go.'

Her lips parted and her eyes gazed searchingly out to sea, like those of a prisoner under sentence of death.

'We'll have to go, then,' she repeated. 'But what's the use of going? What's the use of not going? Nothing makes any difference.'

The thoughts of both turned to the Jallons' garden, to tea and tennis. They thought, in the purity of their frenzied love, of the game they must play, for yet another to-morrow, in the guise of laughing children, and both felt worn out with fatigue.

'Only a few more days, and we'll be parted' – Philippe again took up the burden of his thoughts. 'We'll no longer wake up under the same roof, and I shan't see Vinca except on Sundays, either at home, or at her father's, or at the movies. And I'm sixteen! Sixteen and five make twenty-one. Hundreds and hundreds of days. . . . A few months in the hols, it's true; but then their last few days are always nightmarish. And to think that she belongs to me! That she's mine!'

It was then he noticed Vinca slowly slipping away from his shoulder. With eyes tight shut, she was slipping quietly, imperceptibly, deliberately, down the slope of the rocky ledge, so narrow, that her feet were already dangling over space. . . . He grasped the situation and felt no fear. He deliberated on the timeliness of her action, then tightened his arm round her waist so as never to be parted from her. As he pressed Vinca close, he was conscious of the full living reality, resilience, and vigorous perfection of her young body, ready to obey him in life, ready to drag him down with her to death. . . .

'Death! But what's the use of dying? . . . Not yet. Must I go down to the nether world without having really possessed all this, this girl who was born to be mine?'

On that sloping rock he dreamed of possession as a timid youth might dream, but also as an exacting man, as an inheritor grimly resolved to enjoy the fruits appointed him by time and the laws of man. For the first time it was for him to decide the fate of their future as lovers, and, as master of that fate, to choose whether to abandon her to the waves or plant her firmly on that jut of rock, like the stubborn seeds that flourished there with so little encouragement.

Tightening his arms round her like a belt, he hoisted up the graceful young body so heavy to hold, and woke her by calling out a brief 'Come along now, Vinca!'

She gazed up at him as he stood over her, and seeing him firmly resolute and impatient, it dawned on her that the hour for dying was over. With rapturous indignation she found the setting sun reflected in Phil's dark eyes, on his ruffled hair, on his mouth, and on the shadow in the shape of two small wings of virile down above it, and she cried out, 'You don't love me enough, Phil, you don't love me enough!'

He longed to say something, but all words failed him, for he had no stock heroics to offer her. He blushed and hung his head, guilty – at the moment when Vinca was slipping towards the bourne where love is powerless to torment its victims prematurely – of having treated his little friend as flotsam, as a precious bottle sealed upon a secret that alone was of importance, and of having refused to relinquish her to death.

6

FOR some days past, in the mornings, the scents of autumn had been drifting down as far as the sea.

These late August mornings smelt of autumn from day-break till the hour when the sun-baked earth allowed the cool sea breezes to drive back the then less heavy aroma of threshed wheat, open furrows, and reeking manure. A persistent dew clung sparkling to the skirts of the hedgerows, and if, about noon, Vinca came upon a fallen aspen leaf, the white underside of its still green surface would be damp and glistening. Moist mushrooms poked up through the earth and, now that the nights were chillier, garden spiders retired in the evening to the shed where the playthings were kept, and there wisely took up their abode on the ceiling.

But the midday hours were free of the wisps of autumn mists and of the gossamer threads stretched over bramble bushes laden with blackberries, and the season showed every sign of going back to July. High in the sky the sun sucked up the dew, rotting the morning's mushrooms and smothering with wasps the antiquated vines and their puny clusters. Vinca and Lisette, out walking together, threw off with identical gestures the light woollies that since breakfast had protected their upper arms and bare necks, brown against the white of their frocks. A succession of fine days followed, calm, windless, and cloudless except for the milky 'mare's tails' that trailed slowly across the noonday sky only to vanish into thin air: days so divinely akin to each other that Vinca and Philippe, at peace, almost believed the year to be ending at its sweetest moment, softly held in check by an August that would last for ever.

Under the spell of physical well-being, they thought less often of their September separation and were quit of the moody dramatics, induced at too tender an age, fifteen and sixteen, by their premature love, by the secrecy and silence it imposed, and by the bitterness of their periodic partings.

Many of the young friends, who had joined them for tennis or fishing, had left the coast for Touraine; the neighbouring villas were emptying; Philippe and Vinca remained at the seaside, in the big house where the varnished wood in the hall made it smell like a ship. They enjoyed perfect seclusion in the midst of relations whom they bumped into at all hours yet never noticed. Vinca, concerned as she was with Phil, still carried out all her duties as daughter of the house. In the wild garden she picked bunches of viburnum and fluffy clematis for the table, and in the kitchen garden the first pears and the last black-currants. She poured out the coffee, held a lighted match for Phil's father or her own, cut out and sewed little frocks for Lisette, and lived a strangely remote life among the ghostly throng of relatives whose faces she barely distinguished and whose voices she hardly heard; it was as if she were passing through the agreeable first stages of semi-blindness and semi-deafness that precede a trance. Her younger sister Lisette alone escaped the common fate and shone out in her own true colours. As far as that went, Lisette was as like the Periwinkle as a button-mushroom is to a bigger one.

'If I die,' Vinca once said to Philippe, 'you've always got Lisette. . . .'

But Philippe had shrugged his shoulders and had not laughed, for sixteen-year-old lovers admit neither change, nor illness, nor unfaithfulness, and refuse to countenance death, except to regard it as a reward, or as the decree of fate in the last resort, when no other means of escape can be found.

On the loveliest of these late August mornings, Phil and

Vinca decided to desert the family table and take their lunch and bathing things packed in a picnic-basket, as well as Lisette, on a day's outing. In previous years they had often gone off alone, like explorers, to eat out of doors in one of the deep clefts in the cliffs: a time-honoured pleasure, at present in danger of becoming a doubtful one, owing to their state of uncertainty and misgiving. But this most radiant of mornings bid fair to rejuvenate the two young waifs, who sometimes turned back querulously towards the gate through which they had left the garden of their childhood.

Phil led the way down the coast guard's path, carrying the shrimping-nets for the afternoon's fishing and the string-bag, in which the litre of sparkling cider clinked against the smaller bottle of mineral water. Next came Lisette, wearing a pullover on top of her bathing-dress and swinging in a napkin a loaf still hot from the oven. Vinca brought up the rear, dressed in short white ducks and a blue sweater, and laden with panniers like an African donkey. At all the awkward corners Phil, without turning round, shouted 'Hold on, I'll take one of the baskets!', to be answered by Vinca 'Don't bother!' And, loaded as she was, she contrived to direct Lisette when the high bracken threatened to submerge the small head and its crown of stiff yellow hair.

They chose their chine, little more than a fault in the rocks, where the outgoing tide had spread a carpet of fine sand, a flat cornucopia widening out to the sea. Lisette took off her sandals and began to play with the stranded shells. Vinca rolled up the white ducks over her sunburnt thighs and dug a hole in the wet sand to keep the bottles cool.

'D'you need any help?' Phil asked a little feebly.

She did not deign to reply, but looked at him in silent laughter. For a moment the rare blue of her eyes, the warm bloom on her cheeks that resembled espalier nectarines, and the double curved strip of her teeth, irradiated such a flash of unidentifiable colours that Phil felt as if transfixed. Then she turned away, and he watched her moving about effortlessly, bending down with the free, unhampered agility of a boy.

'It's easy to see that all you've come here for is to feed your face,' she shouted. 'Oh, you men!'

The 'man' of sixteen accepted the implied flattery of this sudden sally. He called out sternly to Lisette when the feast was spread, ate the sandwiches buttered by Vinca, drank his cider neat, dipped his lettuce and his cube of gruyère in the salt, and licked the juice of the runny pears from his fingers. Vinca watched over the proceedings like a young cup-bearer, her forehead bound by a blue fillet. She boned the sardines for Lisette, portioned out the drinks, peeled the fruit, all before quickly settling herself down to eat with huge bites of her strong young teeth. The receding tide whispered low in the distance, a threshing-machine droned drowsily above their heads, and close at hand a thread of fresh water, smelling faintly of the earth, trickled from the rock fringed with grass and tiny yellow flowers. . . .

Philippe stretched out to full length and tucked one arm under his head.

'How lovely it is,' he murmured.

Vinca, on her feet, busied over drying the knives and glasses, let the flash of her blue eyes fall on him. He did not stir, and hid the pleasure he always felt when under her admiring glance. He was aware of the handsome picture he must present, with a flush on his cheeks, a sparkle on his lips, and his forehead pillowed on a fine disorder of raven locks.

Vinca resumed her squaw-like chores without a word, and Philippe closed his eyes, lulled by the ebbing tide, the faraway chimes of a church-clock striking twelve, and the subdued hum of Lisette's little snatches of song. He fell at once into a light sleep, a siesta sleep, pierced by every sound yet weaving each into the pattern of a persistent dream: lying on the yellow sands after a nursery lunch, he was at one and the same time an ancient savage Phil, stripped of everything, but richly endowed in that he possessed a wife.

A shriller cry caused him to raise an eyelid: down by the edge of the sea, drained of all colour by the vertical rays and dazzle of the noonday sun, Vinca was bending over Lisette, attending to some scratch or removing a splinter from a small confiding upstretched hand. The vision in no sense disturbed the trend of his dream, and he once more closed his eyes. 'A child. . . . That's right, we've got a child.'

Philippe's primeval dream, in which love, by outstripping the requisite age for love, surpassed the generous limits of its own boundaries, had plunged him far back among solitudes where he was lord and master. He wandered past a grotto – a slung hammock hollowed by a naked form and the embers of a wood fire flickering at ground level – before the power of divination deserted him and the wings of his imagination were clipped, and he plummeted headlong down till he touched the cushioned depths of deepest sleep.

7

'I simply can't bring myself to believe that the days are drawing in!'

'Why can't you? You say the same thing every year precisely at this season. But if it's changing the solstice you want, Marthe, I'm afraid you have no say in the matter.'

'And where does the solstice come in, I'd like to know? I ask nothing of the solstice, and I expect it to return the compliment.'

'The ineptitude of some women at grasping certain facts is really most curious. Here's one, for example, to whom I must have explained the tidal system at least twenty times, yet her mind is a blank wall when faced with the syzygy!'

'You may be my brother-in-law, Auguste, but I see no reason why I should pay more attention to you than to anyone else....'

'Heavens above, it's small wonder to me you've never found a husband, Marthe!... My dear spouse, would you mind passing me the ash-tray?'

'And if I do pass it to you, where d'you suppose Audebert's going to knock out his pipe?'

'Don't cudgel your brains over my little problems, Madame Ferret. There are plenty of those shells that the children leave about on every table.'

'You're the one to blame for that, Audebert. Ever since you told them that ear-shells are pretty things and would make artistic ash-trays, their scrambles over the rocks have been transformed into a special mission. Isn't that so, Phil?'

'Yes, Monsieur Ferret.'

'It was for that very mission your daughter abandoned

36

her first attempt at money-making, Ferret. Would you believe it? Vinca had the bright idea of coming to some arrangement with Carbonieux – he's the big seed-merchant and bird-fancier, you know – by which she would supply him with cuttlefish for his canaries to sharpen their beaks on. Say at once if I'm telling a fib, Vinca!'

'No, Monsieur Audebert.'

'She's got a better eye for business than she's been given credit for, the little sly-boots. I feel like reproaching myself. . . .'

'Please, Auguste, don't start on that over again!'

'I shall start on it over again if I think fit to do so. Here's a child you require should be kept at home, good. What scope does that allow her for moral and physical activity?'

'Why, the same scope as myself. You don't often find me twiddling my thumbs, I believe! And then, of course, I shall marry her off. That's my one aim in life.'

'My sister's a stickler for the old traditions.'

'Husbands are never the first to complain of that.'

'No truer word . . . Madame Ferret! A girl's future . . . I know time is not of the essence. Fifteen! Vinca has plenty of time to discover her own vocation. . . . Isn't that so, Vinca? Are you listening? Prisoner-in-the-dock, what have you to say in your defence?'

'Nothing, Monsieur Audebert.'

' "Nothing, Monsieur Audebert!" That attitude isn't going to get you very far. I must say, Ferret, our children pay precious little attention to us! An ominous calm seems to be brooding over them this evening.'

'They've been leading such a madcap existence. Vinca, one might almost say, has lost the seat off her pants.'

'Marthe!'

'What d'you mean "Marthe!"? Just because I mentioned the word "pants". We're not English, I'd have you know!'

'Not in front of a young man.'

'There's no young man here, there's only Phil. What are you drawing, Phil?'

'A turbine, Monsieur Ferret.'

'Here's luck to the future engineer, say I! Audebert, have you noticed the moon over the Grouin? For the past fifteen years I've watched the August moon rising over the sea and my eyes have never grown tired of the sight. When one thinks that fifteen years ago the Grouin was bare rock, and that the wind alone is responsible for sowing all those little trees . . .'

'You're telling me the story, Ferret, as though I were a tourist. Fifteen years ago I was hunting along this coast for some little spot where I could blew the first wad of notes I'd ever managed to save.'

'Was it really as long ago as that? Philippe must have been a mere toddler. . . . My dear spouse, do come and take a look at the moon. I don't suppose, in all these fifteen years, you've ever seen her quite the colour she is to-night. She's . . . she's green, I swear it, positively green.'

Philippe turned an inquisitorial eye on Vinca. The talk had been of a time when she, though seen by none, might yet be said to have been in the land of the living. . . . He himself, naturally, had no very clear recollection of the days when they had toddled together on the yellow holiday sands: the midget form of that period – white muslin, brown skin – had faded from his memory. But when he said in his heart of hearts 'Vinca!', the name, inseparably linked with his friend, evoked the memory of sand, warm to kneel on, or trickling out between fingers that held it in a tight squeeze. . . .

The periwinkle eyes caught Phil's, and, inscrutable as his, looked away again at once.

'Vinca, aren't you going up to bed?'

'Not just yet, Mummy, if you don't mind. I'm putting the finishing touches to Lisette's rompers.'

She spoke softly, and then re-entered the world shared by herself and Philippe, leaving outside it the pale, almost non-existent Shades of the family circle. Phil, after drawing his turbine, an aeroplane propeller, and the mechanism of a milk-separator, sketched in on each of his propeller blades a large shadowy eye like that on the wing of a peacock butterfly, before adding several delicate legs and antennae. Then he traced a capital V, and with the aid of a blue pencil transformed this into a blue eye fringed with long lashes – Vinca's eye.

'Look, Vinca!'

She bent forward, put a hand that might have been carved from mahogany – a Red Indian hand – on the out-stretched paper, and smiled.

'How silly you are!'

'What's he done now?' asked Monsieur Audebert.

The two young people turned toward the voice with a look of rather haughty surprise.

'Nothing, Papa,' Philippe replied. 'Just doodles. I've added legs to my turbine to make it go faster.'

'When you show the first streak of intelligence, I'll chalk it up on the mantel. The boy's still six, not sixteen!'

Vinca and Philippe smiled out of politeness and once more banished into outer darkness the vague beings who were playing cards or stitching so close beside them. They still overheard, as though catching the sounds above a bab-bling brook, the gist of some jesting remarks about Philippe's 'vocation' – clearly destined for mechanics and electrical appliances – and on Vinca's matrimonial prospects. An ex-plosion of laughter all round the table greeted the suggestion of marrying her to Phil. . . . 'Ha, ha, ha! It would be just like a sister marrying her brother. They know each other far too well.'

'Love, Madame Ferret, comes unawares, like a clap of thunder.'

'*L'amour est enfant de Bohème*. . . .'

'Marthe, don't sing, please! Not when we're all so keenly enjoying our fill of fine weather, and the nor'-wester. . . .'

. . . An engagement between Vinca and himself! A smile of pitying condescension played over Philippe's features. An engagement! What would be the use? Vinca belonged to him and he belonged to Vinca. In their wisdom, they had already discounted any troublesome effect a long-dated official announcement might have on their age-old passion for each other. They had anticipated the daily jokes at their expense, the intolerable smirks, as well as their own attitude of resistance. . . .

. . . Together they had reclosed the peep-hole through which they sometimes communicated with the world of reality from the fastness of their love. In like manner they each envied their respective parents their childishness, their easy laughter, and their faith in a rosy future.

'How cheery they seem!' Philippe said to himself, as he scanned his father's greying temples for some sign of enlightenment, or at least some trace of a scar. 'Oh,' he decreed pontifically, 'he's never really been in love, the poor man!'

Vinca did her best to imagine a time when her mother, still in her teens perhaps, had suffered, and in silence, the pangs of secret love. She could see her only as she was now, hair prematurely white, gold-rimmed pince-nez, and the slight, elegant figure, which was Madame Ferret's most distinctive feature . . . And she blushed on reaching the conclusion that she, and she alone, had suffered the shame of having to endure the physical and mental torments of being in love. Then she quitted the realm of unreal Shades to rejoin Philippe on the road where perforce they had to cover their tracks, and where they felt they might all too easily perish under the weight of a booty too rich, too burdensome, and one acquired too early in life.

8

AFTER turning the corner into the side road, Phil leapt from his bicycle, flinging it down on the near side and himself on the grass of the chalky verge opposite. 'I've had enough! I'm beat to the wide! What in the world made me offer to take that telegram?'

The eight mile stretch from the villa to Saint-Malo had not seemed to him too unbearable. A following breeze had sped him along, and while coasting down the two long declines a cool shaft of disturbed air had struck sharp against his bared chest. But the return journey had made him fed up with the summer, the bicycle, and his readiness to run errands. August was going out in flames. Philippe scrabbled his legs on the yellowing grass and licked the flinty road dust off his lips. Then he lay flat on his back, spread-eagling his arms above his head. The temporary constriction in his lungs had given him black patches under the eyes, so that he looked as if he had just come out of a boxing ring, while the number of holiday weeks and of days spent in rock-fishing were scored in white scars and black or red bruises on legs that were bronze right up to the line of his scanty running shorts. 'I should have brought Vinca along,' he thought half in jest, 'what a hullaballoo there'd have been!'

But a second Philippe, the one who worshipped Vinca, the Philippe ensnared in the toils of premature love like an orphan prince within the walls of a too vast palace, answered the wicked Philippe, 'You'd have carried her all the way home on your back, if she'd so much as uttered a word of complaint.' To which the wicked Philippe replied, 'That's not at all certain!' and, this time, the loving Philippe dared not pursue the argument.

He was lying beneath a garden wall overhung by blue pines and white aspens. Philippe knew the map of the coast like the back of his hand, had known it ever since he had learned to walk on his two legs or balance between the two wheels of a bicycle. 'This must be Ker-Anna. I can hear the dynamo that makes the electric light. But I've no notion who's rented it this season.' On the further side of the wall an engine was lap-lapping like the tongue of a panting dog, and the silver aspen leaves, twisted the wrong way by the wind, resembled ruffled wavelets. At peace with the world, Phil closed his eyes.

'You certainly look as if you deserve a glass of orangeade,' said a tranquil voice.

Opening his eyes, Phil saw above his head, like an inverse reflection mirrored in a pool, the face of a woman leaning over him. From upside-down, her features presented a too fat chin, lips artificially reddened, the tip of a nose with close-set, irritable nostrils, and a pair of sombre eyes which had the shape of twin crescents thus viewed from below. The whole face, light amber in colour, was smiling with a familiarity far from friendly. Philippe recognized it as belonging to the Lady-in-white, whose car had foundered in the sand on the sea-wrack road, the lady who had addressed him first as 'young fellow' and then as 'Monsieur'. He sprang to his feet and greeted her with all the politeness he could muster. She was leaning over the wall on crossed arms left bare by her short-sleeved white dress, looking him over from head to foot, as on the first occasion.

'Tell me, Monsieur,' she interrogated him in all seriousness, 'is it due to some vow or your own inclination that you wear no clothes, or practically none?'

Philippe felt his cooled-off blood mount in a burning up-rush to his ears and cheeks.

42

'Certainly not, madame,' he cried shrilly, 'it's because I had to bike to the post office with a telegram to one of papa's clients; there was nobody else in the house ready and it would never have done for Vinca or Lisette to be sent out on a day like this!'

'Don't take it so tragically,' said the Lady-in-white. 'I'm fearfully susceptible. The very least thing and I dissolve into tears.'

Philippe was hurt by her words and by her inscrutable stare, for behind it seemed to hover the ghost of a smile. He snatched up his bike by the handle-bars, much as one pulls back a stumbling child by the arm, and was about to jump on to the saddle.

'Do let me offer you a glass of orangeade, Monsieur Phil. It's no trouble, I assure you.' The screech of an iron gate grinding on its hinges reached his ears just as he rounded a bend in the wall, and his attempt at escape landed him up exactly opposite an open door, a double line of hectic pink hydrangeas, and the Lady-in-white.

'My name is Madame Dalleray.'

'And mine's Philippe Audebert,' said Phil with a gulp.

This she waved airily aside with an 'Oh!' of indifference, as much as to say it held no interest for her.

She walked by his side, and endured without flinching the flaming sun on the lustrous coils of her black hair. He began to feel dizzy, and thought it due to a sun-stroke when he once again began to feel, in the presence of Madame Dalleray, a similar fear, and a similar hope, that he might faint and thus be spared the agony of thinking, choosing, and having to obey.

'Totote, the orangeade!' Madame Dalleray called out.

Phil shivered and came to himself. 'The wall's over there – it's not so very high. I'll leap over it and . . .', but he refrained from adding . . . 'I shall be saved.' As he went up the dazzling front steps in the wake of the white dress, he summoned to his aid all the insolence of his sixteen years. 'After all, she's not going to eat me! It's just that she's so set on getting rid of her precious orangeade! . . .'

He followed her indoors, and thought he was going to trip over his own feet when he entered a dark room, closed against sun and flies. The low temperature created by latched shutters and drawn curtains made him catch his breath. He knocked his foot against something soft, collapsed in a heap on a cushion, heard a demoniacal little titter coming from he knew not where, and nearly broke into tears of anguish. An icy tumbler touched his hand.

'Don't drink it all at once,' said the voice of Madame Dalleray. 'Totote, you were crazy to put ice in it. It was cold enough from the cellar.'

Three fingers of a white hand were dipped into the glass and as speedily withdrawn. The sparkle of a diamond glittered in the ice-cube held between the three fingers. Philippe shut his eyes and, with a tightening of the throat, took two sips but tasted nothing, not even the acidity of the oranges. On opening his eyes by then accustomed, he dimly discerned the red and white upholstery, the black and dull gold of the curtains. A female he had not before noticed was leaving the room, carrying a tinkling tray. A red and blue macaw, on a perch, spread one of its wings with the snap of a fan, to display pink underfeathers, the hue of livid flesh.

'How handsome he is!' Phil said in a hoarse voice.

'All the more handsome for being a non-talker,' said Mme Dalleray.

She had seated herself at some distance from Philippe, and there rose between them a thread of vertical smoke from an incense-burner that permeated the room with fumes of resin and geranium. Philippe crossed one bare leg over the other, and the Lady-in-white smiled, to add to the atmosphere of nightmarish luxury, of startling uncertainty, of equivocal rape, so that Philippe was left without a stitch of composure.

'Your people come every year to this part of the coast, do they not?' said the soft, masculine voice of Mme Dalleray, breaking the silence.

'Yes,' he sighed, overwhelmed.

'It is, I must say, a delightful countryside, and one I was not acquainted with at all. Temperate for Brittany, too, hardly characteristic; but restful, and the colour of the sea is beyond compare.'

Philippe did not answer. He was gathering what wits he had left to combat his progressive exhaustion, and expected to hear at any moment a regular, muffled drip-drip on the carpet as the last drops of his life-blood ebbed from his heart.

'You're in love with it all, are you not?'

'With whom?' he asked, almost somersaulting off his chair.

'This coast round Cancale?'

'Yes . . . '

'Are you not feeling well, Monsieur Phil? No? That's good. I'm a very efficient nurse, I must inform you. . . . But, on such a hot day, I couldn't agree with you more – far better to stay still and not talk. So let's not talk.'

'I never said that . . . '

Ever since they had entered the darkened room, she had not made a move nor risked a remark that was not perfectly conventional. Yet each time he heard the sound of her voice, Philippe was afflicted with a sort of inexpressable trauma, and the threat of complete silence filled him with terror. His exit was pitiful and desperately contrived. He knocked his glass against a phantom small table, gave voice to a word or two he never heard himself speak, stumbled to his feet, clove his way to the door through heavy seas and past invisible objects, and was at his last gasp by the time he re-emerged into the light of day.

'Ah...' he managed in a whisper, as he pressed a pathetic hand to that part of the breast where we believe our heart to beat.

Then he quickly pulled himself together, laughed like a half-wit, gave Mme Dalleray's hand a cavalier shake, picked up his bike, and was gone. At the top of the last incline he found an anxious Vinca waiting for him.

'But what in the world have you been doing that's kept you so long, Phil?'

He kissed her on the eyelids, and behind them kissed the lovely blue of his sweetheart's eyes whose deeper shade they only served to enhance, before he answered exuberantly.

'What have I been doing! Why every sort of thing, what do you expect? I was set upon at the turning off the main road, shut up in a cellar, given powerful potions to quench my thirst, tied naked to a stake, tortured, put to the test...'

Vinca laughed as she leaned against his shoulder, while Philippe gave a shake of the head to detach from his eyelashes two tears caused by his nervous strain, and thought to himself, 'If only she knew the truth of every word I've been telling her...'

9

EVER since the day when Mme Dalleray had given him a glass of orangeade, Phil had felt the shock, the burning sensation of the iced drink on his lips and at the back of his throat. Also he began to imagine that never in his life had he drunk, and never again would drink, any orangeade so bitter. 'And yet it had no taste at all while I was drinking it. It was after . . . a long time after . . . ' and the visit, kept a secret from Vinca, started to fester in his memory like a sensitive, throbbing spot, while its fever was amenable to being soothed or inflamed according to his mood.

Philippe's whole life belonged to Vinca, to the darling of his heart, born so close to him in time, a twelve-month after, attached to him as a twin sister is to her twin brother, and as anxiously concerned about his well-being as a mistress over a lover who must leave her the following day. But dreams, and nightmares most certainly, are not controlled by what happens in real life. A bad dream, a dream rich in lurid reds, velvety blacks and golds, and glacial shadows, was beginning to impinge on Phil's life. The normal hours of his day were being diminished by his dream segmentally, as by an eclipse, ever since, one torrid afternoon in the *salon* at Ker-Anna, he had drunk the orangeade poured out by the grave and gracious Lady-in-white. The flash of her diamond at the edge of the glass . . . the die of glittering ice between her three pale fingers . . . the blue and red macaw, silent on its perch, the plumage of its crooked wing lined with white and peach-pink. . . . The poor fellow began to doubt his memory when it so constantly heightened these images by painting them in false and glowing colours – the décor a creation of sleep, perhaps, for sleep deepens to blue the tonal value of leafy greens, and adds sensational highlights to certain other shades.

He had derived no sense of pleasure from his visit. The very memory of the perfumes distilled by the incense-burner, on one occasion, had paralysed his appetite and induced a nervous aberration. 'Vinca, don't you think the shrimps have a whiff of balsam to-day?'

Pleasure indeed! What pleasure had there been in his entry into the darkened room, bumping up against those soft and velvety objects! Or in his clumsy exit, with the hot sun like a cape thrown suddenly round his shoulders! No, no, the very reverse; so far from resembling pleasure, it was more like torture, like the continual embarrassment of an unredeemed debt . . .

'I really must repay her by some act of courtesy,' he said to himself one morning. 'There's no reason why she should take me for a blundering dragon. I must take her some flowers, and then never give her a further thought. But what kind of flowers?'

The long-stemmed marguerites in the kitchen garden, and the velvety snap-dragons, seemed to him contemptible. The last days of August had seen the end of the wild honey-suckle flowers and of the Dorothy Perkins' trained round the aspen boles. But somewhere among the dunes, between the villa and the sea, lay a hollow brimful of sea-holly – blue in flower, mauve the length of its breakable stalks – a flower worthy of being called 'the mirror of Vinca's eyes'.

'Sea-holly, of course. . . . I saw some in a big copper vase at Madame Dalleray's. . . . *Can* one present a bouquet of sea-holly, though? I'll hang them up on the wrought-iron gate. . . . I won't go in. . . .'

In the wisdom of his sixteen years, he waited for a day when Vinca, seemingly none too well, but looking tired and listless and a little on edge, with mauve rings round her eyes, went to lie down in the shade in preference to going for a walk or a bathe. He picked and tied up in secret a bunch of the finest flowers, tearing his fingers to pieces on their iron foliage. He set off on his bicycle in soft Breton weather, that veiled the earth in a ground-mist and mixed an immaterial milkiness in the blue of the sea. He pedalled along, hampered by his white linen trousers and his best woollen stockinnet jacket, till he reached the wall of Ker-Anna; then, crouching low, he crept along as far as the gate, where he longed to chuck his prickly bouquet over into the garden, as though ridding himself of a convicting piece of evidence. He worked out his best plan, crept back to where the surrounding wall almost touched the villa, and, curving his arm like a sling, he slung the bunch up into the air.

He heard a cry, footsteps running on the gravel, and a voice muffled with anger, which he none the less recognized, shouting, 'If I can lay my hands on the idiot who did that . . .'

Feeling insulted, he gave up all idea of running away, and an infuriated Lady-in-white found him just outside the gate. She changed her expression when she saw who it was, stopped frowning, and gave a slight shrug.

'I might have known as much. . . . It wasn't so very naughty after all.'

She waited for an apology which was not forthcoming, since Phil, lost in contemplation of her, was inwardly offering up thanks that she was once again dressed in white, and had added a discreet touch of rouge to her lips and pencilled a dark halo round her eyes. She raised a hand to her cheek.

'Look, I'm bleeding!'

'So am I,' said Philippe roughly, and he held out his lacerated hands. She bent over and squeezed a tiny pearl of blood on to one of their palms.

'Did you pick them for me?' she inquired casually.

He responded with no more than a nod, deriving a rustic kind of pleasure from behaving uncouthly in front of a lady so well-mannered and kind. But she showed neither annoyance nor surprise.

'Would you care to come in for a moment?'

He answered as before, and his mute refusal sent a flurry of hair flying out all round a face, at the moment devoid of all expression other than a strange severity.

'They're such a marvellous blue . . . a blue that's indescribable. . . . I'll arrange them in my big copper.'

Phil's features relaxed a little.

'That's just what I was thinking,' he said, 'or perhaps in a grey-stone pot.'

'Yes, if you like. . . . In a grey-stone pot.'

Philippe was amazed by the note of docility in Mme Dalleray's voice. Noticing this, she looked him straight in the eyes, before she resumed her easy almost masculine smile and changed her mode of approach.

'Tell me, Monsieur Phil. . . . Answer me just one simple question. Did you pick these lovely blue flowers especially for me, to give me pleasure?'

'Yes. . . .'

'How very kind. To give me pleasure. . . . But were you thinking more particularly of the pleasure it would give me to receive them – now listen carefully – than of the pleasure it gave you to pick them for me and present them to me?'

He did not listen properly, but stared at her like a deaf-mute, paying more attention to the words as they formed on her lips and to the flutter of her eyelids. He failed to grasp the meaning of her words and answered at random.

'I thought they would be nice for you to have . . . besides, you offered me your orangeade. . . .'

She removed the hand she had put on his arm, and pushed the half-closed gate wide open.

'Quite so. My boy, you must go away, and never return here again.'

'What?'

'Nobody asked you to be nice to me. So forget the kindly solicitude that brought you here to-day, to bombard me with sea-holly. Good-bye, Monsieur Phil. Unless . . . '

She leaned forward challengingly against the scrolled iron-work of the gate she had so promptly shut between them, and looked at him quizzically as he stood rooted to the roadway.

'Unless, one fine day, I find you on this spot again, having come back, not to repay me for my orangeade with a bouquet of prickly flowers, but for another reason. . . . '

'Another reason?'

'How your voice echoes mine, Monsieur Phil! Next time we shall see whose pleasure is involved, yours or mine. I care only for starvelings and beggars, Monsieur Phil. So, if you do come back, come back empty-handed. . . . Now be off, Monsieur Phil! Shoo!'

She left the gate, and Philippe went off. Turned away, banished even, he still retained his manly pride and, in his memory, the vision of the black arabesques of the gate, like a branch of viburnum, mottling the face of a woman tattooed with the stigmata of her own fresh blood.

IO

'You'll trip up, Vinca, your espadrille's come untied. Hold on. . . .'

Phil bent down briskly, snatched hold of the two white tapes to cross them over a trembling ankle, brown and dry-skinned, the leg of a well-bred filly, conditioned to racing and jumping. Hardened skin and multiple scars did not detract from its shapeliness. With little flesh to cover the bone structure and just sufficient muscle to ensure the proper curve, Vinca's leg could not be said to excite desire, but rather the specialized appreciation of a connoisseur.

'Hold on, I tell you! How can I tie it if you will keep on going?'

'No, let go!'

Her bare linen-shod foot, as if winged, slipped from the fingers that held it and cleared Phil's head as he knelt before her. He caught a whiff of lavender, of well ironed linen and seaweed, the components of Vinca's particular brand of scent, and then saw her standing three paces away. She looked him up and down, shedding on him the dark troubled light of her eyes, whose blue never changed like the inconstant colours of the sea.

'What's got hold of you now? There's no end to your moods. I don't know how to tie a shoe, is that it? I promise you, Vinca, you're becoming impossible!'

Phil's chivalrous attitude was hardly in keeping with the offended look on a face that appeared cast in the mould of a young Roman god's, gilded by the sun, set off by a crown of black hair, its grace impaired only by the faintest shadow –

the fluffy down of to-day, to-morrow's stiff hairs – of a nascent moustache.

'What's the matter? Did I hurt you? Have you got a thorn in your foot?'

She shook her head in prompt denial, let her body relax, and dropped to the ground among the meadow salvia and pink knot-grass, pulling the hem of her frock down as far as her ankles. Her every movement was governed by a quick and pleasing angularity, by a natural poise so exceptional that it would have rejoiced a choreographer's eye. Her happy and exclusive companionship with Phil had trained her to tomboyish games, and to a rivalry in sport as long-lived as her love and not yet undermined by it. There were still times when they could forget their love, despite the force that daily increased its tentacle hold and slowly but surely sapped their mutual trust and gentleness; and despite their very love itself, though it was changing the essence of their tender affection as coloured water changes the complexion of the rose that drinks it.

Philippe did not long submit to Vinca's gaze, though the deep clouded blue of her eyes harboured no resentment. Surprise alone was apparent there, and she was breathing fast, just as a hind, startled by a stroller in the forest, stays hesitantly poised instead of bounding away. She was questioning her own instincts and not the kneeling youth whose clutches she had fled, and it dawned on her that she had just obeyed an impulse of revulsion inspired by distrust and not by false modesty. There was no question of false modesty in a love as great as hers.

She had been quick to apprehend a feminine presence in Philippe's life, warned from the outset by the vigilance of her pure love. She could be said almost to have sniffed the air around him, as if he had been smoking in secret or eating forbidden sweets. She put an end to their talks with a silence as conclusive as a leap, or a look as sudden and weighty as a punch. Whilst they were strolling hand in hand along the road before dinner, she had untwined her shorter, more delicate, fingers from his, and withdrawn her hand from his friendly grasp.

Philippe had found some difficulty in concealing from Vinca his third and fourth visits to Mme Dalleray. But what can walls and distances avail against invisible antennae which, when the heart is enamoured, are extended, sensitive to touch and feel, and, on detecting a blemish, are retracted. His small parasitic secret, attached to their own greater secret, was a blot perhaps on Philippe's scutcheon, yet left him untarnished by any smirch of moral delinquency. Vinca now found him gentle, whereas, by virtue of the despotism of his brotherly love, he should have treated her as his slave. Something of the amenity of erring husbands had crept into his behaviour and made him suspect in her eyes.

After roundly scolding her for acting so strangely, this time Philippe kept up his air of bravado and made his way back to the villa, though it was all he could do not to break into a run. Should he, he wondered, set off in an hour's time to enjoy the hospitality of Ker-Anna, as Mme Dalleray had begged him to do? 'Begged' was hardly the appropriate word for one who knew only how to issue orders and, with dissimulating firmness, dress down the recruit she had a mind to raise to the rank of starveling and beggar. A rebellious beggar, none the less, since he refused to be humbled and, once outside the sphere of her influence, might prove disloyal to the dispenser of cooling drinks, the peeler of luscious fruits, whose white hands were ready to tend and succour the well-set-up young novice who had stopped by her gate. But could he be termed a novice, this youth who since childhood had been dedicated to a love that would keep him pure till he attained to man's estate? Where she thought to find an easy victim, willing to submit to her enchantment, Mme Dalleray discovered an enthralled but doughty opponent. For all the show of outstretched hands and parched lips, this beggar did not display the mien of a subjugated foe.

'He'll always be on his guard,' she surmised. 'He's keeping himself from me.' Mme Dalleray had not yet reached the stage where she could say, '*She*'s keeping him from me.'

On reaching the house, Philippe found it in him to shout back to the sandy meadow where Vinca was still sitting. 'I'm off to the second post. Anything I can do for you?'

She replied with a negative shake of the head that turned her evenly cut hair into a gilded nimbus, and Philippe leapt on to his bicycle.

Mme Dalleray was not expecting him, or so it seemed, for he found her reading. He felt assured of his welcome, however, when he saw the studied half-light in the *salon* and noticed the almost invisible table from which rose a pervasive aroma of slow-ripening peaches, of red cantaloup melon cut in slices the shape of crescent moons, and of black coffee poured over crushed ice.

Mme Dalleray put down her book, and held out a hand without rising. Through the gloom he discerned the white dress and the white hand: her dark eyes, remote in their bistre halo, were more languid in their movement than usual.

'I hope you were not asleep?' Phil said, forcing himself to a conversational opening.

'No.... Certainly not.... Is it very hot? Are you hungry?'
'I don't know....'

He sighed, sincere in his indecision, overcome from the moment of setting foot in Ker-Anna by some kind of thirst, by a susceptivity to the esculent smells that might have amounted to hunger had not his throat at the same time been constricted by a nameless anxiety. His hostess had risen to serve him, and soon he was sipping, from a small silver shovel, the sugar-sprinkled, anis-flavoured red flesh of the melon.

'Are your relatives enjoying good health, Monsieur Phil?'

He stared up at her in surprise. She looked slightly distraught and did not appear to have heard her own voice. He scooped up a spoon in his cuff and it fell on the carpet with the plaintive tinkle of a small bell.

'Clumsy! Just you wait . . .'

She caught hold of his wrist with one hand, and with the other she rolled up his sleeve as far as the elbow, keeping a firm grip on his bare arm with her hot hand.

'Let me go!' Phil cried in a piercing tone.

He jerked his arm away so violently that a saucer broke in pieces at his feet. The echo of Vinca's 'Let go!' shrilled through the buzzing in his ears, and he turned to Mme Dalleray with a glare of questioning fury. She had not moved, and the hand he had cast aside so roughly lay open on her lap like a hollow shell. It took Philippe some little time to weigh up the significance of her motionless attitude. He let his head drop forward, and in front of his eyes passed an incoherent vision of two or three self-images, in which he was either swimming ineluctably through the air, as one flies in dream, or plunging headlong down, as in a dive, at the very moment when the ripples rise up to strike the down-turned face; and then, without enthusiasm, but with deliberate slowness and calculated courage, he put his bare arm back into her open hand.

I I

SOME time about one-thirty in the morning Philippe parted
from the Lady-in-white.

Before leaving the family villa, he had been careful to
wait till all noise and light had been extinguished. The
french window that fastened on a latch, the barred gate that
yielded to his push – beyond those lay the road to freedom.
Freedom! He had walked on foot to Ker-Anna with a
heavy heart, stopping every now and again to drink in a
deep breath, when he would raise and lower his head like a
dog baying the moon. At the top of the final crest he had
turned round to glance back, half-way down the cliff, at the
house where his parents lay sleeping – his and Vinca's, and
Vinca herself. The third window along . . . the little wooden
balcony . . . she would be asleep by now behind the two
closed shutters. . . . In sleep she would be turned a little to
one side, her face on her arm, like a child hiding its tears,
her even hair like an open fan stretching from neck to cheek.
How many times since their nursery days had he watched
her asleep! How well he knew that gentle, rather sad, look
on her sleeping face!

The fear of waking her telepathically had soon made him
turn back to the road, lying white under the milky radiance
of the moon in her first quarter, thus making his way plain.
He had felt reasonably certain of the suspension of his true
love and its attendant anxieties, for even in the depths of his
youthful sleep these still persisted, and never remained very
far below the surface. Their weight, far more than the
glacial fear that grips a young sixteen-year-old on the road
to his first amorous adventure, their weight alone had threat-

ened to turn his journey into a forced march, and – who could tell? – his pride in the delights ahead into a spunkless curiosity! But he had remained poised for no more than a moment before plunging forward again, with much the same antics of shortage of breath and appeals to the moon, as he had pursued his way down the further slope of the hill, which on his return journey, he was to climb more slowly.

'Two o'clock.' Philippe counted the strokes with one ear cocked toward the village clock. The four crystalline quarters, followed by the two graver notes, travelled softly through the warm, salty mist. He added, as a ritual, 'The wind must have veered, you can hear the church chimes and that means a change in the weather,' and the sound of the familiar phrase came to him from far away, from a world that had turned a full circle. . . . He sat down on the grassy edge of a flower-bed in front of the villa, and burst into a flood of tears; he felt ashamed of his tears only at the moment of realizing that he was enjoying a good cry.

Somebody close beside him fetched a heavy sigh: the caretaker's dog, hidden in the shadows at his feet, was dozing on the sandy path. Phil bent over and stroked the shaggy coat and hot nose of the friendly creature who had not barked at him.

'Fanfare . . . good old Fanfare. . . . ' But the dog, who was old and of a Breton disposition, shuffled off out of reach to settle down again with the sound of an old sack.

Every few seconds the slack-water, slumbering under the mist at the foot of the links, sent a little extenuated wave rippling up the beach with the sound of a wet sheet being folded. Not a bird was astir, except for a little owl, which teasingly imitated the mew of a cat, now from the spindle-wood hedge, now from the top of an aspen whiter than the mist.

Slowly, Philippe began piecing together the familiar but still unrecognizable features of the landscape. The stilly night, which frees man's spirit, offered him refuge and the necessary transition between his old life – the happy land of all his summers – and the world now newly opened to his eyes, with its whirl of indistinct, ever-shifting colours and scents and lights, whose concealed source could be as sharp as a dart or spread a pale restricted sheen. . . . Here all was topsy-turvy, the furniture disporting deer-like extremities, the flowers displaying the fluffy undersides of their leaves, their stiff stalks rigid in clear water. Treacherous place, treacherous atmosphere, where a woman's hand or mouth, at will, had the power of loosing destruction on a quiet world, a catastrophe glorified – as are the heavens when spanned by a bridge of light after thunder – by the arched bow of a bare arm.

At least he was leaving behind all the torments so recently endured. He had come away with no more than a swimmer's lassitude, and a survivor's vague and all-embracing sense of comfort on feeling the ground firm beneath his feet. More fortunate than many a young man of his age who, to his lasting hurt, barters a prolonged agony, fraught with limitless visions, against a momentary pleasure that must thereafter curb his dreams, he had returned in a stupor induced by mere lack of sleep; conscious, as a man who has drunk his fill is conscious, that he had only to move to feel rumbling inside him the chilled residue of wine from which the light intoxicating headiness had evaporated.

Day was still far distant, but already one half of the night sky was much lighter than the other. Some very small creature, a hedgehog or rat, ran pattering past as if scratching the ground. Forerunner of the dawn, the first breath of wind bowled a few petals along the path, only to relinquish them and vanish, when all became still again. From the distant steeple the chimes of three o'clock drifted dreamily, the first close and limpid, the other two muffled in a gust of wind. A pair of curlew passed above Philippe's head, low enough for him to hear the straining of their taut wings, and their plaintive cry from over the sea struck deep down in his open and defenceless memory to the very heart of his fifteen blameless years, spent moored to a golden strand and to a growing child who carried her golden head as upright as an ear of corn.

He rose to his feet in an effort to identify himself physically, to force the self who had sat down there to rest – beside the white barred gate, beside the sleeping dog – to be the same self who, the previous night, had turned his face fearfully toward Ker-Anna while leaning on the white gate, while giving the sleeping dog a parting pat. But he could not.

He put his hot hands to his face and felt them to be softer than was usual. They still carried vestiges of a scent so volatile that it vanished under his nostrils when he most wished to establish its essence, yet hung in the air like that of certain sweet-scented plants when their leaves are bruised. At that instant a light shone bright aslant the slats of the shutters in Vinca's room, and a little later went out. 'She's not asleep. She's just looked at the time. Why isn't she asleep?'

He knew, as certainly as if he could see through the walls, how by stretching out her arm Vinca had turned on her bedside lamp to look at the small watch hanging from her brass bedstead, and how, after turning it out again, she had thrown back her head on the pillow, her hair smelling of lavender soap like a well-cared-for child's. He knew, because the night was sultry, that her sunburnt shoulder would be bare, gartered with a thin white strip where protected by the shoulder-strap of her bathing-dress, and, with his mind's eye on her long vigorous body – a body he had watched every year as it grew in beauty – he was struck with sudden stupefaction.

What was there in common between her body, between what love would be able to make of it before it attained its inevitable perfection, and the ultimate destiny of another female body, dedicated to the gentle art of kidnapping, instrument of a relentlessly passionate enchantress, who, in the hypocritical guise of an instructress, was adept in despoiling green untutored youth?

'Never again!' he said out loud.

Only the day before he had been working out, with patient heart, how long it would be before Vinca belonged to him. Now, so much paler after an assignation that left his body as weak and trembling as though he had been defeated in battle, Philippe recoiled in his whole being before a vision so rapacious.

'Never again!'

Dawn was breaking rapidly. But there was no wind to chase away the salty mist over which the roseate light was gaining by leaps and bounds. Phil went into the villa and up to his room, without making a sound. He found it filled with the heavy night air, and as he hurried to open the shutters he was confronted in the glass by his own reflection as a man. . . .

He saw a face drawn with fatigue, two tired eyes, their pupils enlarged, lips still smeared from contact with a rouged mouth, black dishevelled hair straggling over forehead – all signs of distress, resembling less traits of a man than those of a violated girl.

12

At the moment when Philippe finally fell asleep, the sagacious goldfinches were already twittering for the handfuls of seed thrown them by Vinca early each morning. Their sharp cries penetrated his fitful sleep and, in his half-dreams, were transmuted into strips of thin metal ripped from an agonizing helmet clamped to his skull. By the time he was fully awake, the too bright day resounded with the clucking of hens, the buzz of bees, and the drone of the threshing-machine. The sea was turning to green, ruffled by a fresh nor-wester, and beneath his window a white-frocked Vinca stood laughing.

'What's the matter with him? What can be the matter with him? Hi there, Phil! Are you down with sleeping sickness?'

And all round her the Shades, almost as inconspicuous as an old mark on the wall, as ivy or lichen, the Shades, regarded with indifference by the two young people, could be heard re-echoing her words: 'What's the matter with him? What can be the matter with him? He must have been chewing poppy-seeds.'

He looked down on them from the height of his window. His mouth was half-open, giving an affectedly simple look of horror to a face so pale that Vinca's laugh died on her lips, extinguishing that of the others.

'Oh, are you really ill?'

He recoiled from the window as though she had chucked a pebble at him.

'I'll soon show you whether I'm ill or not! But first tell me the time!'

Below him the laughs tuned up again.

'It's a quarter to eleven, sleepyhead! Come on down and bathe!'

He nodded his agreement, but once he had shut the window again and the tulle-curtained panes obscured the daylight, he felt an urge dragging him back towards the night abyss, from which the eddying ghost of a memory, dark and insidious, paraded among the luminous blobs that floated upwards to the full light, there to assume the colour of gold and flesh-tints, or the sudden flash of a moist eye, a ring, a finger-nail.

He tore off his pyjamas and impetuously pulled on his bathing-slip; but instead of going downstairs, as he usually did, half-stripped, he took care to knot the cord of his bathrobe.

Vinca was waiting for him on the links, peacefully letting the upper part of her legs and her sleeveless arms bake in the full sun to the brown of farmhouse bread. The incomparable blue of her eyes under the faded blue foulard filled Philippe with a thirst for cold water, and a yearning for the briny and the off-water breeze. At the same time, he could not help noticing the strength of a body growing each day more feminine, the delicate oval of her knees under their hard exterior, the lengthy muscles running down her thighs, and the proud curve of her back. 'How she's filling out!' he thought.

They dived in together, but whereas Vinca exuberantly splashed her arms and legs about in the listless waves and spouted water as she sang, Philippe, white to the gills and struggling against the shivers, swam with clenched teeth. He stopped swimming the moment Vinca's bare feet touched one of his, sank like a stone, and reappeared only some few seconds later; but he indulged in no reprisals and had recourse to none of their usual pranks, the shouts and jousts and seal-like frolics that made their morning bathe the happiest hour of the day.

They came ashore on a strip of warm sand and enjoyed a thoroughly good rub down. Vinca picked up a pebble and aimed it at a little jutting reef with such accuracy that Phil was grudgingly astonished and forgot that his young play-mate's proficiency in all tomboyish games was due to his own instruction. He felt soft-hearted, outside himself some-how, a feeling akin to weakness, and not a spark of masculine arrogance betrayed the fact that he had fled the house of his childhood, the previous evening, to hasten to his first love affair.

'It's twelve o'clock, Phil. Can't you hear the church clock striking?'

Vinca was on her feet, squeezing the last drops from the even tips of her wet hair. In her first few steps towards the villa, she trod on a small crab that crackled like a cob-nut, and Phillippe was shocked when his heart cockled.

'What's wrong?' Vinca asked.

'You've just crushed a baby crab.'

She turned back, and the sun shone full on her peach-brown cheeks, her lovely eyes, on her teeth and their sur-rounding pink.

'What if I did? It's not the first, by any means. And you don't seem to mind baiting the nets with bits of dissected crab!'

She ran on ahead, and cleared at a bound a hollow in the dunes. For the fraction of a second he saw her suspended in mid-air, her body strained forward, feet together, and her hands outstretched, as if she wished to gather an armful of air.

'I used to think she was tender-hearted,' Philippe mused.

The memory of his nocturnal adventures, that lay doggo during the noonday hour and barely stirred in the depths of its dark lair, was kept at bay throughout the family lunch, where he had to put up with compliments on his poetic pallor and criticism of his loss of speech and appetite. Vinca gobbled up everything put before her, and radiated a maddening cheerfulness. Phil looked at her with hostility, and took full note of the way she cracked the lobster claw with her strong hands, and flung back her hair with a haughty toss of the head.

'I suppose I ought to be thankful,' he thought. 'She suspects nothing.' But he was suffering, all the same, from her imperturbable serenity, and in his heart of hearts he was determined that she ought to be trembling like a blade of grass, horror-stricken by a betrayal which, in all conscience, she should have sensed floating in the air, as she would one of the latent storms that are apt to break, in summer, over any part of the Breton bay.

'She says she loves me. She does love me. Yet she was far more concerned *before* . . . '

After lunch, Vinca danced with Lisette, to the sound of the gramophone. She also insisted that Philippe dance too. She pored over the tidal charts, made ready the nets for the low tide at four o'clock, set Philippe and the whole villa in commotion with her schoolgirl shrieks for the tarred string and the old pocket-knife, and spread, wherever she went, the smell of iodine and seaweed that permeated her patched old fishing-sweater. Philippe, feeling lax, and about to succumb to the sleep which follows close upon major disasters and all great happiness, kept a vindictive eye on her activities, and nervously clenched his fists.

'It wouldn't take more than two or three words to put a stop to all this!' But he knew that he would never bring himself to speak the two or three words, and in his lassitude he longed to go to sleep in a hollow of the warm dunes, his head on Vinca's lap.

Fishing the length of the foreshore, they came upon shrimps, and gurnards that extend their fan-like fins and puff out their rainbow gullets to intimidate their aggressors. But Phil went in passive pursuit of the smaller fry offshore and in the rock-pools. The glare from the mirrored sun hurt his eyes, and he slithered like a novice on the gluey patches of bladder-wrack. They captured a lobster, and Vinca raked about furiously in front of a conger eel's 'hide-out'.

'He's at home all right, you can see!' she shouted, showing him the tip of her iron hook stained with pinkish blood.

Phil turned white and shut his eyes.

'Let the poor creature alone!' he said in a stifled voice.

'The idea! I bet you I get him. What's wrong with you, anyway?'

He was doing his best to hide some inner pain he did not fully understand. What were, then, the fruits of his last night's victory in the scent-laden darkness, in the arms of one so eager to make him a man and proud of his conquest? Surely not the privilege of suffering such tortures, of fainting from weakness in front of an innocent, hardhearted girl! The privilege of trembling so inexplicably in front of feeble, delicate creatures and the sight of their spilt blood!

His next breath almost choked him and, covering his face with his hands, he burst into tears. He was so shaken by his sobbing that he had to sit down, while Vinca remained on her feet, gripping the blood-stained hook as though it were an instrument of torture. She stooped over him, asking no questions, but listening with a musician's trained ear to the new cadence that gave his sobs an intelligible meaning. She put out her hand to touch his forehead, but withdrew it before she touched him. The expression of bewilderment on her face gave way to one of severity, to an ageless grimace, bitter and sorrowful, an altogether virile contempt for the enigmatic weakness of the boy in tears. She carefully picked up the raffia basket in which her catch was flapping about, then her fishing-net, slipped the iron hook under her belt like a sword, and, without turning back, made off with a firm step.

13

HE did not see her again till close on dinner time. She had changed out of her fishing clothes into the pink-scolloped frock of blue crepon that so exactly matched her eyes. He saw that she was wearing white stockings and black suede shoes, and this Sunday attire disturbed him.

'Are there guests for dinner?' he asked one of the family Shades.

'You've only to count the places,' the Shade replied with a shrug.

August was nearing its end, and already they were dining by lamp-light, with the door open on to the green sunset, where a spindle of coppery pink still floated. The sea was asleep, deserted, blue-black as the wing of a swallow, and during the breaks in conversation they could hear the tired, regular lap-lap of slack water. As they sat surrounded by the Shades, Philippe tried to catch Vinca's eye so as to test the strength of the invisible thread that had bound them together over so many years and had preserved them, pure and happy, from the melancholy that falls like a dead weight at the close of meals, at the close of the season, at the close of the day. But she never raised her eyes from her plate, and the light from the hanging lamps lent a polished glow to her rounded eyelids, the curve of her brown cheeks, and her small chin. Then it was that he felt himself abandoned and turned to look – beyond the peninsula, shaped like a couchant lion surmounted by three twinkling stars – for the road, white under the moon, that led to Ker-Anna.

A few more hours, a little longer of the ashy blue in the sky that lends the sunset a smattering of dawn, still a few more ritual phrases: 'Now, now, it's ten o'clock. Don't you children realize that we go to bed at ten in these parts?' and 'I've done nothing out of the ordinary, Madame Audebert, yet somehow I feel as if I'd been on the go all day. . . . ' Still another clink or two from the pantry, the sharp rattle of dominoes on the bare table, yet another squeal of protest from Lisette who, though three parts asleep, would not go up to bed. . . . Still one last attempt to regain contact by a glance, by a secret smile of confidence and understanding from the mysteriously aloof Vinca, and then the hour would strike, the self-same hour that had witnessed, the previous evening, Philippe's furtive escape. His thoughts went back to it with no definite desire, no set plan, as though he were being driven by Vinca's ill-humour to beat a hasty retreat to another refuge, to seek a more welcoming shoulder, to find the warmth and comfort so urgently required by a young convalescent from pleasure, utterly crushed by the passionate hostility of a girl too young.

One by one the rites were accomplished; a maid came to bear away the whimpering Lisette and, on the polished surface of the table, Mme Ferret deposited the double-six.

'Are you coming outside, Vinca? It's awful the way these moths will batter themselves against the lamps!'

She followed him out without a word and, beside the sea, they still found the bright glow that twilight allows to linger there a longer while.

'Wouldn't you like me to go and fetch you your scarf?'

'No thanks.'

They walked side by side, bathed in the thin bluish vapour scented with wild thyme that rose from the links. Philippe refrained from taking her arm, and was horrified at his discretion. 'Oh God, what has come between us? Are we lost to each other? Since she doesn't know what took place *over there*, perhaps I have only to forget it myself for us to be as happy, and as unhappy, as before, and to be as one again.'

But to these wishful thoughts he did not add his belief in hypnotism, for Vinca was there walking beside him, cold and gentle, as if her great love had deserted her and left her unreceptive of her companion's anguish. And all the more because he himself felt his *hour* imminent, and was beginning to tremble in much the same way as when, the day after he had been stung on the arm by a stinging-ray, he had become feverish and experienced the same excruciating pain in the dressed wound when the salt water rose to cover it.

He stopped and wiped his forehead.

'I feel as if I'm suffocating. I'm not well, Vinca.'

'No . . . not well,' the voice of Vinca echoed.

Thinking her mood had changed, he was too eager in voice and gesture.

'Oh, how sweet you are! Oh, darling. . . '

'No, I'm not sweet,' the voice interrupted.

The childish phrase left him still some hope, and he caught hold of her bare arm.

'I know what's the matter. You're angry with me because I cried to-day, like a woman.'

'No, not like a woman. . . . '

He blushed in the dark and tried to explain.

'Can't you understand? When you were tormenting that conger in its hole . . . when the brute's blood got on your lobster hook . . . all of a sudden it made my heart turn. . . . '

'Oh I see, your heart . . . turn. . . . '

The tone of her voice was so full of meaning that Philippe caught his breath in dread. 'She knows all.' He waited for the shattering proof, the flood of tears and the moans. But Vinca remained silent, and after a long time, like the period of calm that follows a thunder clap, he risked asking a timid question. 'And was my display of feebleness enough to make you pretend not to love me any more?'

Vinca turned her face toward him, bright under the moon yet a clouded blur between the two stiff hedges of her hair.

'Oh, Phil, I love you all the time. Unfortunately, what you did makes no difference.'

'You mean it? Then you can forgive me for being such a cry-baby, for making such a fool of myself?'

She hesitated for no more than a second.

'Of course I can forgive you, Phil. But there again, it makes no difference.'

'To what?'

'To us, Phil.'

She spoke with the persuasive calm of a prophetess, so that he dared not question her further, or take heart from what he had heard. Doubtless Vinca must have followed the trend of his thoughts to their inmost recesses, for there was subtlety in her answer.

'Do you remember, not three weeks ago, how you worked yourself up into a frenzy – and so did I – because we were both so impatient at having four, perhaps five more years of cooling our heels before we could get married. My poor Phil, I really believe I'd like to go back and be a child again, to-day ...'

He waited, in case she should underline or comment further upon the so cunning, the insidious 'To-day' that hung suspended before him in the blue August night. But Vinca was already practised in the art of silence.

'Then you're no longer angry with me?' he pursued insistently. 'To-morrow we'll be ... we'll be Vinca-and-Phil again, just as we always were? And for ever?'

'For ever, if you wish it, Phil. .... Come, let's go in. It's chilly.'

She had not repeated his 'as we always were', so he had to be content with an incomplete promise and a cold little hand for a moment clasped in his. For, at that precise minute, with the creak of the well-head chain and the clank of the empty pail, with the jingle of curtains along the length of their rod – the last human sounds of the day – Philippe's hour struck, the self-same hour for which he had waited, the previous night, before unfastening the door of the villa and hastening forth unseen. . . . Oh, the dim red glow in that unknown room! Oh, the dark ecstasy, the protracted death, the return to life under slow-beating wings!

As if, ever since the day before, he had been expecting some sort of absolution from Vinca – the ambiguous absolution that she had just pronounced with such sincerity in her voice, such reticence in her words – he realized, quite suddenly, that he was a man and was able to appreciate the gift that a beautiful, authoritative female demon had bestowed upon him.

14

'Is the day of your return to Paris settled yet?' Mme Dalleray asked.

'We know we always have to be back there by the twenty-fifth,' Philippe answered. 'Sometimes, depending on what date Sunday falls, we leave on the twenty-third or twenty-fourth, or maybe the twenty-sixth. But it never varies by more than two days.'

'Really! So, in short, you leave in a fortnight's time. So to-day fortnight, at this time . . . '

Philippe stopped staring at the sea – flat and white near the sands, and far out the colour of a tunny's back under the low clouds – and turned towards Mme Dalleray. She was wrapped in the ample folds of some white stuff such as Tahitian women wear, smoking reflectively, her hair set, her powder matching her skin; and there was nothing about her to show that the young man sitting not far away, handsome and sunburnt as herself, was anything else to her than a younger brother.

'So, in a fortnight's time, at this hour, you'll be . . . where?'

'I'll be . . . oh, in the Bois, on the lake. Or more likely on the tennis-courts there, with . . . with some friends.'

He blushed, for Vinca's name had been on the very tip of his tongue, and Mme Dalleray smiled, the smile he had observed before, that gave her the appearance of a handsome lad. Philippe turned back to the sea, if only to hide his face, which showed the resentful petulance of an angry young god. A deliciously soft but firm hand was placed on his. Whereupon, without his gaze ever leaving the desultory grey sea, an expression of agonized happiness stole slowly up from his relaxed mouth to his eyes, in which the intermittent flash of white and black was finally extinguished behind closed lids.

'You mustn't be sad,' Mme Dalleray said, in a gentle voice.

'I'm not sad,' he quickly protested. 'You can't understand. . . .'

She bent her head so beautifully lustrous.

'You are right. I can't understand. Not everything.'

'Oh . . .'

Philippe gazed in awe, in reverent mistrust, at the woman who had revealed to him a terrifying secret. Did a low cry still re-echo in her small pink ears, like the smothered cry of someone whose throat is being cut? When he had felt light and on the point of fainting, her two arms, deceptively so much stronger than they looked, had borne him from this to another world; and her two lips, so sparing of words, had pressed upon his lips to impart a single all-powerful word, intoning an indistinct chant that was but a feeble echo rising from the depths of chaos and old night. . . . She knew everything. . . .

'Not everything,' she repeated, as if Philippe's silence required an answer. 'But you don't like my asking you questions. And sometimes I am a little tactless. . . .'

'Like a flash of lightning, yes,' Philippe thought. 'When it forks zigzagging across the sky, it does throw light on things that otherwise remain in shadow, even in broad daylight. . . .'

'And all I wanted to ask you was whether you'll be very pleased to leave me?'

The young man looked down at his bare feet. A loose-fitting garment of embroidered silk gave him the appearance of an Indian potentate and accentuated his good looks.

'What about you?' was his schoolboy retort.

The ash of the cigarette Mme Dalleray was holding between her fingers dropped to the carpet.

'I don't come into it. This is a question that concerns Philippe Audebert and not Camille Dalleray.'

He looked up at her in surprise on hearing once again this name which could belong to either sex. 'Camille. . . . Yes, of course that's her name. Well, she can keep it as far as I'm concerned. To myself I always call her *Madame Dalleray*, the *Lady-in-white*, or plain *She*.'

She was still smoking at her leisure and staring out to sea. Could she be called young? Yes, she could certainly be called young. Thirty to thirty-two. Inscrutable, as are all calm persons, the extent of whose facial expression never goes further than a tempered irony, a smile, a certain gravity. Without turning away from the stretch of sea over which a storm was brooding, she once again put her hand on Philippe's and squeezed it, entirely for her own pleasure and with little thought for him. Under the pressure of her small powerful hand, he spoke, constrainedly, yielding up his confession, as a squeezed fruit oozes its sweet juice.

'Yes, I shall be sad. But I hope I shan't be unhappy.'

'Really? And why do you hope so?'

He gave her a feeble little smile, looking shy and touching, just as, secretly, she would have wished him to be.

'Because,' he answered. 'I think you'll arrange something. Yes, I'm sure you'll arrange something.'

She lifted one shoulder, raised her Persian eyebrows. It required an effort on her part to force her smile into its habitual mould of serene disdain.

'Some . . . thing . . . ' she repeated, 'that means, if I understand you correctly, that I am to invite you round to my place, as I do here, if I still wish to, whereas all you have to do is to join me there whenever your school . . . and family ties permit?'

He showed surprise at the tone, but still held the eye of Mme Dalleray.

'Yes,' he answered. 'What else should I do? Do you blame

me? I'm not a little go-as-you-please vagabond. And I'm only sixteen and a half!'

The colour mounted slowly to her cheeks.

'I don't blame you for anything. But don't you imagine that any woman . . . any woman but me, that is, might well be shocked when she knew that all you wanted was one hour alone with her – that only, only that?'

Phil was listening to her with the loyal attention of a schoolboy, his eyes wide open, staring at her reticent mouth and at her jealous eyes, which, however, made no demands of him.

'No,' he said, without hesitation, 'I can't conceive of you're being hurt by what I said. "Only that?" Please, only that. . . .'

Then words failed him and the colour left his cheeks, confronted once again by concern for his future happiness, and Camille Dalleray's placid effrontery wavered as she computed the measure of respect she owed to her handiwork. Philippe, as though dazzled, let his head fall forward, and his victrix felt momentarily intoxicated by his gesture of submission.

'Do you love me?' she asked in a low voice.

He quaked and looked at her fearfully.

'Why . . . why do you ask me that?'

She recovered her self-control and, with it, her ambiguous smile.

'I was only joking, Philippe.'

He did not at once stop questioning her with his eyes, while inwardly censuring her for the temerity of her words.

'A fully developed man would have said yes in answer to my question,' she reflected. 'But if I insist, this boy will start to cry, and between his sobs and his kisses blurt out that he does not love me. Shall I insist? If I do, then I shall have to dismiss him, or perhaps sit trembling while I learn from his lips the precise limits of my influence over him.'

She felt a painful little contraction in the region of her heart and, as if oblivious of his existence, she rose and wandered aimlessly towards the open bay-window. Through it entered the smell of the small blue mussels, left stranded high and dry at the base of the rocks during the past four hours, and with it the thick heavy scent, reminiscent of an infusion of elderbloom, that rose from the privet hedge in the last stage of its flowering.

As she leaned out with a faraway look, Mme Dalleray was conscious of the presence of the young man lying down in the room behind her, and of the weight of a persistent little desire.

'He's waiting for me. He's calculating the amount of pleasure he can count on me giving him. What I got from him was to be had for the asking by the first passer-by. But this consciously timid, middle-class youth bridles when I ask him about his family, stands on his dignity when he speaks of his school, and immures himself behind a bastion of silence and offended modesty at the mere mention of the name Vinca. . . . He's learnt nothing from me except the easiest. . . . Whenever he comes here, he brings with him, each time doffing and donning it with his clothes, his . . . his . . . !

She realized that she had just hesitated before the word 'love', and she turned away from the window. Avidly Philippe watched her approach. She put her arms on his shoulders, and with a slightly brutal shove she forced his dark head down on to her bare arm. She hastened with her charge towards the narrow confines of the shadowy realm where she, in her pride, could interpret a moan as an avowal of weakness, and where beggars for favours of her sort drink in the illusion that they are the generous donors.

15

A LIGHT but persistent rain during the night had vaporized the salvias, glazed the privet and the motionless leaves of the magnolias, and, without splitting the protective gauze of its covering, bedewed with tiny pearls the nest of the processionary caterpillars in one of the pines. The wind left the sea untroubled but sang under doors in a feeble, rather tentative voice, that brought back memories of the past year and mysteriously suggested ripe apples and roasting chestnuts. At its instigation, as soon as he was out of bed, Philippe put on a dark blue sweater under his linen jacket and came down last to breakfast – a frequent occurrence ever since his sleep was less pure and peaceful, and started later in the night. He hurried off in search of Vinca, as if he longed to find some sunny terrace after skirting a wall deep in shadow; but she was not in the hall, where the moist atmosphere accentuated the strong smell of varnish in the woodwork and of hemp in the hangings, and she was not to be seen on the terrace.

A fine impalpable sea-mist drifted through the air and clung to his skin without wetting it. A yellow aspen-leaf, detached from its branch, hovered for an instant with intentional grace in front of Philippe's eyes, then tipped over and darted earthwards as if impelled by an invisible weight. He cocked one ear and listened to the winter sound of coal being shovelled on to the kitchen furnace. From another room rose a shrill protest from little Lisette that ended in a whimper.

'Lisette,' he called. 'Lisette, where's your sister?'

'I don't know,' wailed a small voice blurred with tears.

A gust of blustery wind whipped a slate off the roof and hurled it crashing at his feet, where Philippe stared at it in stupefaction, as if before his very eyes fate had smashed to smithereens the mirror that brings seven years of bad luck. He became a small boy again, very far removed from good luck. He felt no desire to call out to the woman who, not so far away, in the pine-shadowed villa beyond the promontory shaped like a lion, would have rejoiced, none the less, at any sign of faint-heartedness on his part, or of looking for support from some source of indomitable female energy. He hunted all over the house without a glimpse of his young friend's fair hair or of her frock, the blue of sea-holly, or again of her spongy cotton frock, the white of fresh mushrooms. No long brown legs with delicate dry-skinned knee-caps hastened to meet him, nor could he find a refreshing pair of blue eyes, enhanced by two or three shades of blue with a hint of mauve, to bring comfort to his own.

'Vinca! Where are you, Vinca?'

'Why, in here,' answered a quiet voice close beside him.

'In the shed?'

'In the shed.'

In the cold light peculiar to windowless outhouses where daylight enters only through the door, a crouched figure was sorting through a variety of garments spread out on a dust-sheet.

'What are you up to?'

'You can see for yourself. I'm sorting. I'm checking. We'll soon be leaving, so it's got to be done . . . mother said so.'

She looked at Philippe and then squatted down, crossing her arms over her knees. He found it irritating to see her looking so poor and humble.

'There's not all that hurry! And why do you have to do it yourself?'

'Who else is there? If mother got down to it, she'd soon have a heart attack.'

'But the maid could˝surely . . .'

Vinca shrugged her shoulders and returned to her ploy,

keeping up a low running commentary, just as real seam-stresses do when a swarm of them keep up a busy little buzz like humble bees.

'There, that lot's Lisette's paddlers . . . the blue . . . the green . . . the striped . . . might as well throw them away and have done with it, for all the wear that's left in them. That's my frock with the pink scollops. . . . It might stand one more washing, I suppose. . . . One, two, three pair of espadrilles, all mine. . . . And this pair's Phil's. . . . Another of Phil's. . . . Two old cellular shirts of Phil's. They've gone a bit in the arm, but the fronts are still quite good. . . .'

She held up the openwork garments, discovered a couple of rents in them, and pursed her lips. Philippe was looking at her with no sign of gratitude in his pained and hostile expression. He was suffering from the grey light under the tiled roof, from seeing her so busied, and because he had left his bed too soon. He started to draw a comparison there and then, a comparison which did not originate in the love he concealed and the hours he had spent over at Ker-Anna, nor yet one that included Vinca; Vinca, the whole religion of his childhood, Vinca, deserted, but with all due respect, for the exciting and necessary intoxication of a first love affair.

He started making comparisons then and there, among the old garments spread over a mended sheet, between the four walls of unfaced brick, in the presence of a girl wearing a lavender overall faded on the shoulders. She was on her knees, and only interrupted her task to toss back her trimly-cut hair, kept damp and soft by the daily bathe and the salty air. Over the past fortnight she had lost something of her high spirits; she was much quieter, and her mood of stub-born equanimity was beginning to make Philippe uneasy. Had she, this young housewife with the Joan-of-Arc hair, had she really made up her mind to end her life with him rather than wait for the time when they would be able to love freely and openly? With a frown on his face, he stood

79

measuring the effects of the change that had taken place, and though his eyes were on Vinca, his thoughts were far away. When she was close beside him, the danger of losing her ceased to be real, and he was no longer tormented by the urgent desire to retrieve her. Yet it was on her account that he had begun to make comparisons. His newly acquired capacity for feeling, for suffering at unexpected moments, together with a sense of intolerance bequeathed him by a chartered libertine, flared up at the least provocation. At the same time he felt justifiably disloyal as, with heightened perception, he found himself reproaching the second rate for their second-rateness and their general attitude to life. He was slowly discovering not only the world of emotions which, for want of a better term, we call physical, but also the need for some more material beauty to clothe the obvious imperfections of the neophyte who tended the altar at which he worshipped. He was beginning to hanker for things that were pleasant to touch, to look at, to listen to – velvets and scents and music – for he had now learned to appreciate the rise and fall of a speaking voice. He made no bones about it, since he knew all too well how much better he felt when surrounded by intoxicating luxury, and how a certain garb of oriental silk, slipped over his shoulders in the secrecy and subdued light of Ker-Anna, added to his stature and ennobled his soul.

He was tentatively groping after some vague and generous new plan. Failing to grasp the fact that what he really wanted was a Vinca beyond compare, well dressed and smelling delicious, he was reduced to trying to find out why it grieved him so to find her on her knees, unlovely in her natural simplicity. He gave vent to a few harsh words, to which Vinca paid no heed. He became embittered, and she responded just enough for him to become more insulting, then ashamed of his violence. He devoted a little time and trouble to pulling himself together before he expressed some sort of contrition in phrasing a lame excuse that afforded him a certain pleasure. Vinca, meanwhile, with patient hands, went on tying sandals together in pairs and turning inside out the pockets of cast-off jumpers full of pink shells and skeletal sea horses.

'And what's more,' Philippe said in conclusion, 'it's all your fault. You never answer back. . . . So I go on and on, working myself up and up. . . . You let me damn you into heaps. Why?'

She enveloped him in a look full of feminine wisdom, that overflowed with the wiles and concessions of overweening love.

'All the time you're teasing and tormenting me,' she said, 'at least I have you near me.'

16

'This is where we come to an end this year,' Philippe thought gloomily, as he gazed out to sea. 'Vinca and I together are just sufficiently one person to be twice as happy as either of us singly, and this year the person who is Phil-and-Vinca is going to die here. What a frightening thought! Is there nothing I can do to prevent it? And here I am. . . . And this evening, after ten o'clock, perhaps I shall be off once again to Mme Dalleray's, for the last time these holidays.'

He dropped his head, and his black hair drooped, disconsolate.

'If I had to go off there now, at this very moment, to Mme Dalleray's, I'd refuse to go. Why?'

Under a dismal sun, beset by two serried storm-clouds, the road to Ker-Anna wound like a white ribbon along the flank of the hill, and then disappeared among a thicket of stiff junipers, grey with dust. Philippe turned away, struck by a repugnance which did not deceive him. 'It's all very well. . . . But what about to-night?'

After his third repast at Ker-Anna, he had given up going there every night, from fear of rousing his parent's suspicions and Vinca's qualms. Besides, his extreme youth made him tire of inventing alibis. He began to have his doubts, too, about the potent, clinging scent that pervaded everything in Ker-Anna, and most of all the body, naked or scantily clad, of her whom he had come to refer to in secret – dependent upon his alternating moods, either with the pride of a licentious schoolboy, or the stricken remorse of a husband who has deceived a beloved wife – as his mistress, and sometimes as his 'master'.

'Whether they find out or not, it means the end of us two. Why?'

Among all the many books he had read, propped on his elbows among the dunes or, for reasons of shyness rather than of fear, in the retirement of his own room, there was not one that had taught him that a chap must needs founder in so ordinary a shipwreck. A hundred pages or more of a novel would be taken up by the preliminaries to sexual desire, while the act itself was dismissed in a dozen lines, and Philippe searched his memory without recollecting a single story in which a young man cast off the shackles of childhood and chastity at one fell blow and did not continue to be shaken by strong, almost seismic tremors for many a long day after. . . .

He got to his feet and walked along the edge of the links, where the foreshore had been fretted and frayed by the equinoxial gales, till he came to a low gorse bush in its second flowering that grew leaning toward the beach, held and kept in position by a straggling network of roots. 'When I was young,' he said to himself, 'this gorse bush didn't lean toward the beach. The sea has eaten away the ground between, more than three or four feet of it, while I've been growing up. Yet Vinca swears it's the gorse bush that's moved forward.'

Not far from the furze bush lay the rounded hollow, carpeted with sea-holly, the hollow known as 'Vinca's Eyes' because of the blue of its flowers. It was there Phil had cut a bunch of the finest plants, the prickly tribute tossed over the wall at Ker-Anna. . . . To-day the shrivelling flowers round the rim of the hollow looked desiccated. He stopped there for a moment, too young to smile at the mystic meaning that love lends to a dead flower, a wounded bird, a broken ring. Then, shrugging off his uneasiness and broadening his shoulders, he tossed back his hair with the traditional gesture of pride and cursed himself under his breath with a string of maledictions that would not have marred the pages of a Sunday-school adventure story.

'Come, enough of this shilly-shallying! At all events I can truthfully say, this year, that I've grown to be a man. As for what's to become of me . . . '

He caught himself thinking aloud and blushed. But then, what about his future! A month earlier he had been thinking along similar lines, but a month earlier he had envisaged a future painted in precise and childish detail against a broad vague background – his future and exams, starting his matric all over again, accepting thankless tasks not too ungrudgingly because 'they have to be done, don't they'; his future and Vinca, all the former things made bearable because of her, his future cursed or blessed in the name of Vinca.

'I was hard put to it at the beginning of the hols,' he thought. 'But now!' and he gave a wry smile not unlike that of an unhappy man. Each day his upper lip was becoming more darkly shadowed, since the first fine down – which is to the moustache what a crop of spring hay is to coarse cutch-grass – had lent his mouth a slightly inflamed and swollen look, like a grief-stricken child's. It was to this mouth that Camille Dalleray's inscrutable, almost vindictive glance would return again and again.

'But let's get back to my future! It's perfectly simple. If I don't watch out, it means my father's business – refrigerators for town and country houses, headlamps, spare parts, motor accessories. Once I'm through my matric, then straight to the office stool – invoices, clients, correspondence. Papa just manages to scrape enough out of it to run a car. . . . Oh, I was forgetting my military service. What can I be thinking of! So let's go back and say that once I've passed . . . '

The flow of his thoughts came to a sudden stop, stemmed by an infinite boredom, by a profound indifference to no matter what a future without secrets might hold in store for him. 'If your military service keeps you within easy distance of Paris, then during that time I shall . . . ' At the back of his mind he could still hear the loving little voice of Vinca whispering more than a dozen plans, plans evolved during that very summer, and now lying flat and punctured, without life, substance, or colour. His rosy hopes extended no further than the day's end, dinner time, and a game of chess with Vinca or Lisette – preferably with Lisette, who, aggressively precocious for her eight years, keen-eyed and calculating, solaced his soulful preoccupations – till at last the moment came for him to sally forth, a willing sacrifice to pleasure. 'And besides,' he thought, 'it's none too certain that I shall go. Not by a long chalk! Since I don't behave like a love-sick loony, counting the minutes and for ever turning my head toward Ker-Anna like a sunflower to the light, I can well afford to remain myself, and continue to take pleasure in all that I enjoyed *before*. . . .'

He did not notice that in pronouncing the word 'before' he had firmly established it as a wedge between the two periods of his existence. He could not yet be sure for how long all the past events of his life would come slap up against this stumbling-block, this trite yet miraculous landmark. 'Ah yes, that was *before* . . . Of course, I remember now, that was some time *after*.'

With a contempt tinged with jealousy, he thought of his day-school pals, quaking at the knees as they waited outside the portals of ill-fame from which they would emerge whistling, liars and braggarts, sickened with disgust. Then they would forget all about it, then go back again, with no break in their work, their games, clandestine cigars, debates on politics or sport. 'Whereas I . . . Then it can only be her fault. *She's* to blame for the fact that I no longer desire anything any more, not even *She* herself.'

A 'blanket' of fog, coming from nowhere, enveloped the whole coastline. When over the sea it had been little more than a drifting frayed curtain, hardly thick enough to obscure a rocky islet. All of a sudden a strong stiff breeze had grappled and given it a good bracing, then deposited it pell mell, packed and opaque, over the bay. In a trice Philippe was drenched in fog, with just time enough to observe sea, beach, and villa disappear, before he found himself choking in a vapour bath. Used as he was to the vagaries of the seaboard climate, he waited for the next bracing air stream to dissipate the temporary fog, and resigned himself to his limbo, to his symbolic blindness, in the depths of which gleamed a face, like a full moon, peering from windswept hair, and two idle, gestureless hands. 'She never moves. . . . But oh, let her give me back all that I've lost! The passage of time, eagerness, impatient haste, curiosity. . . . It isn't fair. . . . It isn't fair. . . . How much I grudge it her!'

He worked himself up into a state of rebellious ingratitude. No boy of sixteen and a half can realize that it is in the order of things that fair missionaries are thrown across the path of young men destined by love to be lovers in too great haste to live and therefore impatient to die, and that the blandishments of these sirens cause time to stop, lull the spirit to sleep and rest, and bid the body ripen under their instruction.

The fog blanket suddenly lifted, drawn up into the air like a sheet being lifted from the drying-ground, and leaving behind it a momentary fringe of water on every blade of grass, a pearly dew on all the downy leaves, a wet varnish on the smooth.

The September sun cast a fresh clean yellow light over a sea blue in the distance and turning to green offshore, where sand lay beneath.

Once the sea fog had cleared, Philippe filled his lungs again as joyfully as if he had just come out from a stuffy corridor into the bright sun and air. He turned to face inland, where the gold of the gorse in its second flowering streamed down the rocky chines, and shuddered when he saw a small boy standing close behind him, like a wraith wafted by the fog and left forgotten.

'What do you want, young'un? Aren't you the kid whose mother sells us fish at Cancale?'

'Yes,' the small boy said.

'Was there no one in the kitchen? Are you looking for somebody?'

The urchin shook the dust out of his red hair.

'The lady told me ... '

'What lady?'

'She said to me, "Go and tell Monsieur Phil that I've gone away".'

'What lady?'

'I don't know. She said to me "You'll tell M. Phil that I have to go away to-day." '

'Where did she tell you this? On the road?'

'Yes. . . . In her car.'

'In her car. . . . '

Philippe shut his eyes for a moment and passed his hand over his forehead, letting out a deliberate whistle 'Phe ... ew. In her car. . . . Yes, I see. Phe ... ew.' He opened his eyes again to find his messenger no longer where he had been standing, and at once he was reminded of one of the short-lived dreams, crudely sketched, brutally effaced, that came to him during his after-lunch siestas. But he caught sight of the child of ill-tidings just as he was disappearing along the cliff path, picking him out by his carrotty thatch and the bluish patch on the seat of his pants.

Philippe threw himself into a becomingly foolish posture as if the Cancale urchin could still see him.

'Right, and it doesn't make much odds if she has gone. One day, sooner or later – what's the difference, since she had to leave!'

But he was aware of some strange discomfort, almost entirely physical, in the pit of his stomach. He let himself give way to the pain, inclining his head thoughtfully, as if listening to the mystical words of advice.

'Perhaps on a bike, I . . . But supposing she isn't alone? I never thought to ask the kid if there was anyone with her!'

Somewhere along the coast road a car hooted in the distance. For one brief moment the prolonged blare made him forget his pain, but the next moment he felt his vitals contract, with the cramping effect of a low placed punch.

'At least I don't need to worry whether to go and see her to-night!'

Suddenly he thought of Ker-Anna standing barred and bolted in the moonlight – grey shutters, black gate, imprisoned geraniums – and he shivered. He lay down in a dry fold of the links, writhing like a retriever puppy in the throes of distemper, and began scratching up the sandy turf with regular movements of his two feet. He closed his eyes, for the procession of huge cumulus clouds with their fleecy billowing whiteness brought on a feeling of nausea. He went on and on digging at the sandy turf with rhythmical kicks, in much the same way that a woman in the pangs of childbirth rocks herself to and fro, her groans becoming progressively louder and louder till she gives vent to the final cry.

On opening his eyes, it took him more than a few moments' astonishment to recover his senses. 'What's up? What's wrong with me? I've always known she had to leave before we did. I've got her Paris address and her telephone number . . . so how can it affect me if she's gone! She's my mistress, not my beloved. I can get along without her.'

He sat upright and shelled the tall grass stalks of their string of climbing snails so delectable to cows; he indulged in a coarse laugh and a little ribaldry. 'So, she's quit, good! And I'll bet she's not gone off alone, either, that piece! She was never too keen on telling me about her little love affairs, not she! So there we are. Alone or not alone, she's done a bunk. And what do I lose by it? One night – to-night. One only before we ourselves go away. One night, and I wasn't so sure myself that I wanted to go, a moment since. I was thinking only of Vinca. . . . It simply means we'll have to give up any idea of a pleasant evening, that's all!'

But some kind of cold wind blew over his spirit and swept away all his guttersnipe smirks, his false confidence, his cheap sneers, leaving his mind only with a clean surface, a clear understanding of what Camille Dalleray's departure really meant to him.

'Oh, she's gone away . . . she's gone beyond recall. The woman who gave me . . . who gave me . . . How can I express what it was she gave me? There is no name for it. She just gave. She's the only person who's given me anything since my early days when Christmas used to be so wonderful. Yes, she gave me something, and now she's taken it away.'

The colour mounted to his bronze cheeks and his eyes pricked with tears. He tore open his shirt, ran the fingers of both hands through his hair, made himself look as if he had just left the ring after a gruelling round, panted, and cried aloud in a raucous, childish voice 'And it's just this one more night I wanted most of all!'

Pressing his body up by the wrists, he craned his neck and eyes toward the invisible Ker-Anna: already the bare summit of the hill was overwhelmed by an advance mass of rain-clouds teeming in from the south; and Philippe accepted the fact that some threatening all-powerful Ifrit had expunged from the map the actual spot where he had known Camille Dalleray.

Someone coughed not so very far below him on the crumbling sandy path, where twenty times a year logs and flat stones were fitted to form rustic steps, and twenty times a year tumbled downhill to the beach. Philippe watched, on a level with his eye, a head with greying hair mount into full view; with the genius for dissimulation inherent in every child, he tidied himself up by smoothing away all the wild disorder of a man betrayed, before settling himself to wait, calm and collected, for his father to pass by.

'Ah, so here you are, young fellow!'

'Yes, Papa.'

'All by yourself? Where's Vinca?'

'I don't know, Papa.'

Almost without an effort, Phil was able to keep his face set in the becoming mask of an eager, sunburnt youth. His father, standing before him, looked like his father on any other day: a genial kind-hearted apparition, rather indistinct and woolly round the edges, like all other earthly creatures whose names were not Vinca, Philippe, or Camille Dalleray. Phil waited patiently for his father to recover his breath.

'Haven't you been fishing, Papa?'

'The idea! I've been for a walk. As it happens, Lequerec contrived to land an octopus. It had legs as long as my walking-stick here. Most remarkable. Lisette would have screamed had she seen it. You'd better have a care, all the same, when you're bathing.'

'Oh, there's no real danger, you know!'

Too late Philippe realized that he had answered back on a note too childishly high-pitched and false. The grey, piercing eyes of his father were questioning his; and he could not tolerate for long a look that he found frank and straightforward, from eyes clear of the insolent and protective cloud behind which secret-ridden sons live in the midst of their relations.

'Are you worried by the thought of this departure, young man?'

'This departure! But Papa ...'

'Yes, yes. If you're like me, you'll find it becomes more of a strain every year. The countryside, the villa. And then the Ferrets. ... It's not always so easy – friends with whom one spends the summer each year – not to feel the wrench. Make the most of the time you have left, young man. Another two days of fine weather. There are thousands worse off than you.'

Even while the words were still on his lips, he was drifting back among the shadows whence he had been brought into the open by an ambiguous word and a steady stare. To help him climb the disintegrating cliff, Philippe lent him an arm, with the cold impartial attention a child condescends to bestow on a father, whenever the father is a quiet, middle-aged man, and the son a turbulent youngster, in the first flush of discovering love and its physical torments, and proud to be suffering alone in all the world, and not asking for help.

On reaching the flat, narrow terrace where the villa lay, Philippe let go his father's arm and made as if to go back down towards the beach, wishing to return to the spot chosen within the last hour as his own special corner of human solitude.

'Where are you off to, young man?'

'There, Papa . . . down there below. . . . '

'Are you in a great hurry? Come along here for a moment. I'd like to explain one or two things to you, about the villa. You know we've decided to buy it, Ferret and I, jointly? But of course you know all about it! We've been discussing it long enough in front of you children.'

Phil made no answer, not daring to lie or to confess to the buzzing deafness that cut him off so completely from all family conversation.

'Come along and I'll explain. First, my idea – conjointly with Ferret – is to enlarge the villa by adding on two ground-floor wings, so that the roof will form two flat terraces for the best rooms on the first floor. Do you get the idea?'

Philippe nodded knowingly, and tried his level best to concentrate. But try as he would, he lost his bearings at the word 'corbelling', and his mind slipped back down the slope to where the ill-omened little boy had said . . . 'corbelling . . .

corbelling . . . I got stuck at corbelling.' Yet he kept on nodding his head and glancing, his look instinct with filial attention, from his father's face up to the Swiss chalet roof, and down from the roof to M. Audebert's hand, as it traced the new design in the air. 'Corbelling.'

'You've got the idea? That's what we shall do, Ferret and I. Or perhaps it will be you, in conjunction with the young Ferret girl. . . . For there's no telling who will be spared among us or who will die.'

'Ah, I can hear once again!' Philippe gave an inward shout, turning a mental somersault at his deliverance.

'Do you find that funny? There's nothing to laugh at. You youngsters have no respect for death.'

'But we do, Papa!'

('Death! A familiar word at last – one I can understand. An everyday word.')

'There seems every reason to suppose that you'll marry Vinca, later on. At least that's what your mother assures me. But then again, it's just as probable that you won't marry her. What makes you smile?'

'What you've just said, Papa.'

('What you've just said, and the simplicity of all parents and grown-ups, and of those who, as they say, have lived: their ingenuousness and the disturbing purity of their minds.')

'Please note that I'm not asking for your opinion on that subject at the moment. If you were to tell me you wanted to marry Vinca, it would have much the same effect as if you declared that you did not want to marry Vinca.'

'Would it?'

'Yes. The time's not yet ripe. You're a pleasant enough lad, but . . .'

Once again the piercing grey eyes peered out from the general confusion and scanned Philippe.

'. . . but you must wait. The Ferret girl won't have much more than a bean to her name. But what does that matter?

For the first few years it's easy to do without silks and velvets and gold.'

('Silks and velvets and gold! Oh, the velvet, the silk, and the gold, red and black and white: red, black, white. And the cube of ice, cut like a diamond, in the glass of water. My velvet, my silk, my splendour, my mistress and my master. Oh, how can I do without such luxuries!')

'. . . Work. . . . Hard times to start with. . . . Serious. . . . Plenty of time to consider . . . the age we live in. . . . '

('Something's hurting me. Here, in the pit of my stomach. And I can't stand the sight of that purplish rock against the dull red of the background, black and white, now that I come to look into it more closely. . . . ')

'Family life . . . pampered. . . . *By Jove!* . . . Having a good time. . . . *Steady, young fellow, steady!*'

Voice and intermittent words were swamped in the gentle surge of incoming waters. Philippe knew nothing more, except for a slight shock to his shoulder and the tickle of dry grass against his cheek. Then the sound of several voices, like so many jagged island rocks, again broke through the pleasant, regular, booming of the water, and Philippe opened his eyes. His head was lying in his mother's lap, and all the Shades, in a circle, were bending over him with harmless expressions. A handkerchief sprinkled with lavender water touched his nostrils, and he smiled up at Vinca, as she broke through the barrier of the Shades, gold and rosy amber and crystalline blue. . . .

'The poor pet!'

'Didn't I tell him he wasn't looking at all well!'

'We were both of us standing here chatting: he stood there, right in front of me – when all of a sudden – crash!'

'He's like every other boy of his age, quite incapable of looking after himself, pockets stuffed full of fruit. . . . '

'And now that he's begun to smoke. . . . Do you suppose those first cigarettes count for nothing.'

'My poor darling. His eyes are filled with tears.'

'Of course. It's the natural reaction.'

'What's more, it can't have lasted more than thirty seconds – just the time it took to call you all here. As I was saying, here we are chatting together, and then . . .'

Phil got to his feet, light-headed, his cheeks cold.

'Now do stay where you are. Don't try to walk!'

'Lean on my arm, young man.'

But, with an expressionless smile, he took Vinca's hand.

'It's all over. Thanks, Mother. It's all over now.'

'Wouldn't it be best if you went to lie down?'

'Oh, no. I'd much rather stay out of doors.'

'Do look at Vinca's face, I ask you! Your Phil's not dead yet! Go along, take him with you. But stay on the terrace as long as you can.'

The Shades drifted away, friendly hands and words of encouragement rising from the slow-moving throng; one last flashing smile from his mother and he was left alone with Vinca, who was not smiling. He attempted, with a tilt of the lips and a reassuring nod, to induce a gayer mood, but she shook her head to this without ever taking her eyes off him, staring at the greenish tint that had spread over his tan, at his black eyes with a touch of red in them from the sun, and at his lips parted over small closely set teeth. 'How handsome you are, and how miserable am I!' Vinca's blue eyes seemed to say. . . . But he could read no pity there, and she let him hold her hand, hardened by tennis and fishing, as if she were offering him the handle of a walking-stick.

'Come along,' Philippe urged her in a low voice. 'I'll explain everything. It's nothing, really. But let's go to some quiet spot.'

She went along, and together they chose as their secret chamber a flat slab of rock only occasionally washed over by the highest tide, which left behind it a coarse-grained sand, quickly dried. Neither of them ever dreamed of exchanging confidences behind light cretonne curtains or between pitch-pine partitions, resonant as a musical instrument in that they carried from room to room, at night, the news that one of the inmates of the villa had switched off a light, or coughed, or dropped a key. There was enough of the primitive savage in both these Paris-born children to make them shun the pit-falls of human habitation and seek out some nook – in the middle of an open field, the edge of a rocky fastness, the hollow of a wave – and there conduct their lovers' tiffs and idylls in security.

'It's four o'clock,' said Phil, consulting the sun. 'Wouldn't you like me to fetch you your tea before we settle down?'

'I'm not hungry,' Vinca answered. 'But wouldn't you like something?'

'No thanks. My little dizzy spell has taken away my appetite. You sit down there in the middle, it's better for me to be near the edge.'

They spoke simply, each knowing they were about to embark on a serious conversation, or on an equally revealing period of silence.

Vinca's smooth brown legs, crossed under the hem of her white frock, gleamed in the rays of the September sun. Far below them, a harmless ground-swell, soothed and smoothed by the passing of the heavy fog patch, was beginning to dance and by degrees be decked out in its clear weather finery. Gulls cried overhead, and a string of fishing-smacks hove into sight, sail following sail from behind the shadow of the Meinga to gain the open sea. A shrill, tremulous, childish lilt was borne down past them on the breeze; Philippe turned round, shivered, and a kind of querulous moan escaped him. At the tip-top of the highest cliff, in faded blue crowned with red hair a little boy. . . .

'Yes,' Vinca said, following his gaze, 'that's the little boy.'

Phil recovered himself in time to say, 'You're referring, I suppose to the fisherwoman's little boy?'

Vinca shook her head. 'The little boy,' she said, correcting him, 'who came to speak to you just now.'

'Who came to . . .'

'The little boy who came to tell you the lady has gone away.'

Philippe was seized with a sudden loathing for the dazzling sun, the hard sand so uncomfortable under his body, the breeze burning his cheeks.

'Who . . . what are you talking about, Vinca?'

She disdained to answer, and went on, 'The little boy was looking for you and gave me the message first. So you see . . .'

She let the sentence peter out on a fatalistic gesture. With something approaching a feeling of comfort, Phil took a deep breath.

'Oh, so you knew, then. . . . What did you know?'

'Certain things about you. . . . Not for very long, though. What I knew I learnt all at once, about . . . about three or four days ago, but I can't be sure. . . .'

She broke off and Philippe noticed, where the curve of her fresh childish cheeks began, immediately under the blue of her eyes, the mother-of-pearl traces of sleepless nights spent in tears, the satiny moonshine shadow that is seen only on the eyelids of women constrained to suffer in silence.

'Right,' he said. 'Now we can talk, unless you'd rather not talk. I'll do whatever you wish.'

She repressed a tiny quiver at the corners of her mouth, but no tears flowed.

'No, let's talk. I think it's best.'

From the very first words of their conversation they both felt an identical bitter satisfaction at having overridden the common ground of altercation and fib-telling. Only heroes, actors, and children can perform the feat of feeling at ease on an exalted plane. These two children fondly believed that a noble grief could be born of their love.

'Listen, Vinca, the day I first met her . . .'

'No, no,' she broke in precipitately, 'not that! I beg of you, not that! I know all about it. Down there, on the sea-wrack road. Do you imagine I've forgotten it?'

'But,' Philippe protested, 'there was nothing that day either to remember or forget, since . . .'

'Stop! Stop, can't you! Do you think I brought you here so that you could talk about her?'

From the sharp simplicity of Vinca's tone, he knew his own accents of a moment since must have lacked all semblance of contrition.

'To tell me the whole story of your love affair, that's what you want, isn't it? Don't bother. When you came back to the house last Wednesday, I was out of bed, but hadn't switched on my lamp. . . . I saw you . . . like a thief. . . . It was almost daylight. And what a look you had on your face! I got all the information I wanted then, I can tell you! Do you suppose what goes on along the coast isn't known to everyone? It's only parents who know nothing.'

Philippe was shocked, and showed it in a frown. He was offended by the fundamental feminine brutality roused in Vinca by jealousy. He had felt ready, when climbing up to their hanging refuge, for a few half-confidences, a few tears, more than ready, indeed, for a lengthy confession. But he would not support this wanton flaying alive, this expeditious savagery which was destroying his idea of picturesquely flattering slow stages, and was leading to . . . to what, in fact? 'I can only suppose she wants to do away with herself,' he said to himself. 'She wanted to die here at this very spot one day not so long ago. . . . She's going to wish to die now. . . .'

'Vinca, you must promise me . . .'

She turned to listen without looking at him, and in this slight movement the whole of her body expressed a wealth of ironic independence.

'Yes, Vinca. You must promise me that you'll never try,

either here on this rock or anywhere else in the world . . .
never try to . . . do away with yourself.'

She dazzled him with a flash of blue, staring at him with
wide-open eyes.

'What's that you said? Do away with myself?'

He put his hands on her shoulders and gave her a nod
heavy with experience.

'I know you, darling. Six weeks ago, at this very spot, for
no known reason you wanted to let yourself slide down over
the edge, and now . . .'

All the while he was speaking, her eyebrows rose in a
heightened arc of utter stupefaction. With a twist of her
shoulders she jerked off Philippe's hands.

'Now? . . . Kill myself? . . . Why?'

The last word had made him blush, and she took his blush
for an answer.

'Because of her?' she shouted. 'You must be mad!'

Phil tore scraps of the meagre grass in his frustration, and
quite suddenly looked four or five years younger.

'One would have to be a raving lunatic to try to find what
a woman wants, or to imagine that she knows herself!'

'But I do know, Phil. I know very well. And I also know
what I don't want. You may rest assured I shan't kill myself
on that woman's account. Six weeks ago . . . Yes, I did let
myself slip over the edge there, and I dragged you with me.
But that time it was for your sake I wanted to die, and for
my own . . . for my own. . . .'

She shut her eyes and threw back her head, letting her
voice linger on the last phrase, and, thus, she bore a strange
resemblance to all women who throw back their heads and
close their eyes in an excess of felicity. For the first time
Philippe recognized in Vinca a close kinship to her who,
with eyes shut and head in any position, appeared to separate
herself from him at the very moments he was holding her
closest.

'Vinca! Stop that at once! Vinca!'

She opened her eyes again and sat bolt upright.

'What?'

'Why, don't carry on like that! You look as if you're going to faint.'

'No, I'm not going to faint. You're the one that needs smelling-salts and eau-de-Cologne and all the rest of the bag of tricks!'

From time to time, mercifully, a childish ferocity crept between them. They drew fresh strength from it, becoming steeped once more in anachronistic clearsightedness, before plunging headlong back into the follies of their elders.

'I'm going off,' Philippe said. 'You're making me feel wretched.'

Vinca gave a laugh, the unpleasant staccato laugh of almost any woman wounded in her pride.

'That's rich! So now you're the one who's made to feel wretched, are you?'

'You bet I am!'

She uttered a piercing cry like an irritated bird, so unexpected that Philippe was startled.

'What's wrong?'

She was supporting her body on her outspread hands, crouching like an animal, almost on all fours. He saw that she had suddenly become purple with rage, frantic. The two flaps of her hair were almost touching across her tense face, leaving only a clear glimpse of parched red lips, a short nose dilated by the fury of her breathing, and eyes burning with the blue of a flame.

'Shut up, Phil! Shut up, or I shall hurt you! You dare to say that you are to be pitied, to say that you are wretched, when it's you who deceived me for another woman! You've no shame, no sense, no pity! You brought me here to tell me what you've been doing with another woman. Deny it! Deny it! Deny it if you can!'

She was shrieking on the full flood of her feminine fury, in her element, like a petrel in the teeth of a storm. She collapsed in a heap, but her groping hands happened upon a fragment of rock and this she hurled far out to sea with a strength that astounded Philippe.

'Now be quiet, Vinca!'

'No! I won't! First, we're all by ourselves, and then I want to scream! I've got something to scream about, too, I can tell you! You've brought me up here because you want to tell me, to go back over the whole story of what you did with her, for the pleasure of listening to yourself, of hearing your own words . . . of speaking of her, and saying her name, eh! her name, perhaps . . . '

Suddenly she struck his face a blow so unexpected and so tomboyish, that he only just stopped himself setting about her and giving her a sound hiding. What held him back were the words she had shouted at the pitch of her voice, while his innate sense of masculine decency recoiled before the extent of her knowledge and her brazen use of it.

'She thinks, she really believes it would give me pleasure to tell her. . . . Oh! . . . and it's Vinca, Vinca who's got these ideas in her head!'

She did stop for a moment, speechless and coughing, scarlet from face to bosom. Two small tears brimmed and fell from her eyes, but she had not yet reached the soothing stage of silent crying. 'So I've never known what thoughts were in her mind,' Philippe mused. 'Every word she's said is as great a surprise to me as the strength I've so often noticed when swimming or jumping or when she throws a stone!'

He kept a wary eye on Vinca's movements, feeling none too sure of her. The bright colour of her skin and eyes, the precise outline of her slender figure, the hem of her white frock stretched over her long legs, helped to relegate to some remote sphere the almost sweet suffering that had stretched him, prone, on the grass.

Profiting by the momentary lull, he wished to show proof of his superior self-control.

'I didn't strike you, Vinca. But your words asked for it even more than what you did. But I had no wish to hit you. It would have been the first time I'd ever let myself go to that extent.'

'Of course,' she broke in hoarsely. 'You'd hit anyone rather than me. I never come first in anything.'

He felt reassured by her all-devouring jealousy and able to smile, but her vindictive expression warned him that it was no time for joking. They both remained silent, watching the sun set beyond the Meinga and the splashes of rosy pink, like in-curving petals, that danced on the crest of every wave.

From the cliff-top came the tinkling of cow-bells, and at the point where the ill-omened urchin had passed singing out of sight, a black goat showed its horned head and bleated.

'Vinca, darling,' Philippe sighed.

She looked at him indignantly.

'Do you dare to call me that?'

He bent his head. 'Vinca, darling,' he sighed.

She bit her lip, rallying her strength against the assault of tears she knew to be on their way, since they brought a lump to her throat and swelled her eyes, and did not dare to risk a word. Philippe's neck was supported by the rock patched with a short-napped purple moss, and he was staring out to sea, without, perhaps, seeing it. Because he was tired, because the weather was lovely, because the evening hour, its scents and melancholy, made it imperative, he sighed 'Vinca, darling,' as he would have sighed 'Oh, how happy I am!' or else 'How miserable I feel!' In his present despondent mood, he found utterance in the oldest words of all, the first that came to his lips; just as the war-scarred veteran, grievously wounded, moans in his agony the name of a mother long since forgotten.

'Shut up, you fiend, shut up! What have you done to me, oh, what have you done to me!'

She showed him her face streaming with tears that left no trace on her velvety cheeks. The sunlight played on her brimming eyes and enhanced the deeper blue of their pupils. The upper part of her face shone with all the attributes of a woman in love, hurt past endurance, yet magnificent enough to forgive everything; while her trembling mouth and chin, not uncomic in their quaint grimace, were those of a desperately unhappy little girl.

Without lifting his head from its stony pillow, Philippe turned to look at Vinca, his dark eyes softened by their languishing appeal. Anger had brought out from her overheated body the smell peculiar to all fair-haired women, so curiously akin to that of the pink flower of the restharrow or to crushed green corn, acrid and pungent, and it completed the impression of vigour imposed on Philippe by every gesture she made. Yet there she sat in tears, stammering. 'What have you done to me?', and gnawing a hand on which he could see the mauve semicircular mark left by her young teeth.

'Little savage!' he whispered, with the caressing inflection he might have used to a woman he did not know.

'More so than you'd think,' she answered in similar vein.

'Don't say such things!' Philippe shouted. 'Your least word sounds like a threat.'

'Before, you would have said "like a promise".'

'They're one and the same,' he protested vehemently.

'Why?'

'Because they are.'

He nibbled a blade of grass, determined on prudence, incapable, as it happened, of putting into precise words his cloudy claim to think what he liked, his right to speak the polite and refreshing lie, which his youth and the expansive excitement of his first affair made him long to assert.

'I'm wondering how you're going to treat me, Phil, later on?'

She seemed dismayed, bereft of argument; but Philippe knew her powers of recovery and how speedily, as if by magic, she rallied her strength.

'Then stop wondering,' he begged, shortly.

'Later on ... later on. ... Even the future is under distraint. She's got a nerve; fancy being able to think how the future's going to pan out, at a moment such as this! It's her mania for tying things up that makes her talk like this. She's miles away from any idea of wanting to die!'

In his peevishness, he misinterpreted the will-to-survive vested in the female of every species, and the imperious instinct to wallow in calamity while at the same time working it like a mine rich in precious ore. Abetted by the evening hour and his own fatigue, he felt exasperated by this combative chit, battling as she was in her primitive way for the preservation of their united future. He tore his thoughts forcibly away from her presence, and let them rush off in pursuit of a car as it disappeared behind its cloud of dust and, catching up with it, he gazed like a roadside beggar through the window behind which lolled a head turbaned in white veils.... Once more he looked closely at every detail – the darkened lashes, the small black mole close to the lip, the close-set, sensitive nostrils – traits that he had observed only at close range, oh, so very close! Distraught, terrified, he leapt to his feet, filled with the fear of suffering and with surprise at his discovery that while talking with Vinca he had ceased to suffer....

'Vinca!'

'What's the matter?'

'I ... I think I'm going to be ill!'

An irresistible arm seized hold of his and forced him down on to the safest spot, for he had been swaying on the edge of their perilous escarpment. Knocked out, he had no fight left in him, and said only 'Perhaps it would be the easiest way out after all. . . . '

'Hush, hush, oh hush!'

She sought for no further words after this trite cry. She cradled his enfeebled body against her own and cuddled his dark head against breasts newly rounding out with fuller softer flesh. Philippe relapsed into his recently formed habit of passive lack of resistance acquired in the embrace of another, whose readily accessible bosom and clinging scent he sought in vain; yet in his almost unbearable frustration he still was able to murmur 'Vinca darling . . . Vinca darling. . . .'

She took to rocking him to and fro, knees pressed together and arms folded, swaying with the motion known to every female creature the world over. She cursed him for being so wretched and so spoilt. She longed for him to lose consciousness and forget, in his delirium, a certain woman's name. Inwardly she murmured 'There, there now . . . you'll learn to understand me . . . I'll see that you do,' while outwardly she removed from his forehead a stray black hair, the vein in the marble. She enjoyed testing the weight and the new feel of a young man's body which the day before, running and laughing, she had carried pick-a-back. When Philippe opened his eyes and sought hers, begging her to give him back all that he had lost, she struck the sand beside her with her free hand and cried out in her heart of hearts 'Why, oh why were you born!' like the heroine in an eternal triangle.

And all the while she kept an eagle eye on the house and its immediate surroundings; like a mariner she gauged the time by the setting sun, 'It's after six,'; her roving glance lit on Lisette, like a white pigeon in her fluttering frock, as she made her way back from beach to villa. And she thought 'We mustn't stay here longer than another quarter of an hour or they'll be coming to look for us. Then I must bathe my eyes properly . . . ', before she started to re-assemble body and soul, love, jealousy, slow-cooling anger, sorting them out in the inner recesses a mind as primordial and rugged as their nest among the rocks.

'Get up,' she said in a low voice.

Philippe mumbled a protest and his body grew heavier. She guessed he was grumbling, and making the most of his inertia, to stave off her questions and reproaches. She shook his neck and supine warm body with arms that had been dandling him with a mother's care, and her charge, once freed of her embrace, turned back into the youth who had lied to her, the unknown stranger, capable of betraying her now that he had been smoothed and polished by a woman's hands.

'If I could only tether him, like that black goat, at the end of a couple of yards of rope . . . or shut him up in a room somewhere, my room . . . or live in a land where I was the only woman. Or better, if I were only beautiful, really beautiful . . . or else, that he were just ill enough for me to have to look after him!' The drifting shadows of her thoughts flitted across her face.

'What are you going to do?' Philippe asked.

Snatched back from her day-dreaming, she gazed at features which one day, doubtless, would be those of a handsome enough dark-haired man, but would remain, for his seventeenth year and a little time after, just this side of manhood. She was amazed that no terrifying or revealing mark disfigured the smooth chin or the nose so quick to show anger. . . . 'Oh, but his eyes. His two gentle brown eyes, with their whites a pale blue! Now I know that a woman has admired herself in them!' and she tossed her head.

'What am I going to do! Get myself ready for dinner. And so are you.'

'And is that all?'

Now on her feet, she pulled down her frock under the silk elastic belt, keeping a wary eye on Philippe, the villa, and the sea, that lay grey and cold, ready for sleep, refusing to participate in the glory of the sunset.

'That's all . . . unless you go and do something. . . . '

'Depends on what you mean by something.'

'Oh well . . . disappear, dash off to find that woman again . . . make up your mind that she's the one you love. And announce the fact to your parents.'

She spoke in chilling childlike tones, tugging at her dress as if she wished to eliminate her breasts.

'She's got breasts like clinging limpets, or like those little conical hills in Japanese prints,' and he blushed because, in his thoughts, he had enunciated so distinctly the word 'breasts', and accused himself of lack of respect.

'I shall do nothing of the sort, Vinca!' he blurted out. 'But I'd very much like to know how you'd take it, if I were capable of doing even the half of what you suggest!'

She looked at him open-eyed, but there was no answer he could read in eyes that were all the bluer for the tears they had shed.

'Me! It wouldn't make me change my way of life in the slightest.'

She flung the lie in his teeth, but behind the glaring false-hood in her eyes he came upon the tenacious, restless, un-scrupulous constancy that upholds a woman in love and binds her fast to life and her lover, when once she discovers that she has a rival.

'You're making yourself out to be more level-headed than you really are, Vinca.'

'And you're making too much of yourself. Weren't you saying just now that you thought I'd wanted to do away with myself? Die, because my lord has had an affair?'

She pointed at him with her open hand as children do after a squabble.

'An affair!' Philippe repeated, hurt and at the same time flattered. 'Good Lord, all the boys of my age . . . '

'Then I suppose I must get used to the fact,' she interrupted him, 'that you differ in no way from "all the boys" of your age.'

'Vinca darling, I swear that a girl like you can't speak . . . oughtn't to listen to . . . ' He lowered his eyes priggishly and bit his lip before adding, 'You must believe me.'

He held out a hand to help Vinca leap across the bench-long schistous slabs outside the entrance to their shelter and then over the low whin bushes before they reached the coast guard's path. Three hundred yards ahead they could see Lisette, twirling like a white convolvulus on the links as her midget brown arms signalled to them, semaphoring 'Come on quick, you're late!' Vinca waved back in answer, but again turned to Philippe before starting on her way down.

'Phil, it's simply that I can't believe you. Otherwise the whole of our life up to now has been simply one of those mawkish tales we've read in books we don't much care for. You speak of "A young man, a girl . . . ", when it's ourselves we're discussing. You said to me "An affair like all the boys of my age . . . "; but, Phil, you're making a big mistake, all the same. You see, I'm talking quite quietly.'

He listened to her, a little impatient and perplexed, for at the moment he was finding it hard to recollect all the whips and scorpions of his horrid torment, and found it even harder when he noticed the look of extreme embarrassment behind her bold exterior, and when, to add to his difficulties, the evening breeze sprang up with spiteful malevolence.

'Well, what else?'

'You're making a big mistake, all the same, Phil, because it's me you ought to have asked. . . . '

He wanted no more, weary, longing to be alone, yet full of apprehension at the thought of the long night ahead. She had made allowances for his crying out, or being indignant, or else being heartily ashamed of his questionable behaviour:

he measured her up from toe to top through half-closed eyes and said, 'Poor little mite! It's all very well to say "asked"; but what can you give in return?'

He saw that she was reduced to offended silence, and watched her quick blood mount in a dark flush to her cheeks and then spread down under the sunburnt skin of her neck and throat. He put his arm round her shoulders and walked pressed close against her along the path.

'Vinca darling, you must see what nonsense you're talking. The nonsense of an ignorant girl, thank God!'

'Thank Him for something else, Phil. Don't you realize I know as much as the first woman He created?'

She did not draw away from him but, without turning her head, looked at him sideways, then down at the path ahead, and then again at Philippe, whose attention was riveted on the angle of her eye which, as the pupil shifted, showed alternate white and periwinkle blue, like the nacreous lining of a shell.

'Tell me, Phil. Don't you believe I know as much as . . .'

'Hush, Vinca. You do not know. You don't know anything.'

At the bend in the path they came to a halt. All the azure in the sea had drained into a solid grey metal almost without a ripple on it, while across the horizon the setting sun had left a lengthy streak of discouraging red and above it a pale green zone lighter than the dawn, where the moist evening star glimmered feebly. Philippe tightened his grasp round Vinca's shoulders and with his other arm pointed to the sea.

'Hush, Vinca, you know nothing. It's so . . . It's such a secret. So big!'

'I'm big.'

'No. You don't understand what I'm trying to tell you.'

'But I do, perfectly. You're behaving like that young Jallon boy who sings in the choir on Sundays. He tries to make himself important by saying, "Oh, Latin! Well, you know, Latin's jolly difficult"; but he doesn't know a word of Latin.'

She gave a sudden laugh, raising her head, and Philippe did not like the way, so quickly and so naturally, she shifted from tears to laughter, from dismay to irony. Perhaps because night was falling, he began to assert his claim to a calm haven fraught with smouldering sensual desires, and a silence during which the blood drumming in his ears was like torrential rain; he yearned for the latent fears, the speech-depriving, peril-infested period of subjugation, that made him crouch outside portals which other youths of his age entered reeling and blaspheming.

'Be quiet, do. Don't make it sound coarse and cheap. Once you do know . . .'

'But I'm only asking to be told.'

She spoke the first words that came into her head and giggled like an inexpert actress trying to cover up 'the butterflies'; also because she felt as miserable as all children scorned, who are ready to risk untold hardships on the chance that by suffering a little more, then more still, then still a little more, they will get what they want in the end.

'Vinca, please! You're making me very uncomfortable. That sort of talk is so unlike you.'

He removed his arm from her shoulder and continued on down the path at a faster pace. She kept up with him, avoiding, where the path narrowed, the spiky tufts already wet with dew by jumping over them; as she went along she moulded her features in readiness to face the Shades, all the while repeating in an undertone that Philippe could hear, 'So unlike me? . . . So unlike me? . . . That's one thing that you, Phil, with all your knowledge, do not know.'

Throughout dinner they both behaved in a manner that did credit to themselves and their secrets. Philippe laughed off his 'vapours', required fussing over, and drew attention to himself in his fear that remarks might be passed on Vinca's blazing eyes, red and bruised round the rims, which she did her best to shade under the silky thatch, cut in a thick fringe above her eyebrows. She, for her part, acted the child; she demanded champagne as soon as the soup was on the table – 'to put Phil on his feet again, Maman' – and emptied her glass at one draft.

'Vinca!' scolded a Shade.

'Let her be,' from another indulgent Shade, 'What harm can it do her?'

As the meal drew to an end, Vinca noticed Philippe's gaze wander over the night sea in search of the invisible Meigna, the white road swallowed up by the darkness, the junipers petrified beneath the dust of that road.

'Lisette!' she cried. 'Give Phil a hard pinch, he's falling asleep!'

'She's drawn blood!' Philippe groaned. 'The little pest, she's brought tears to my eyes!'

'It's true, it's true,' Vinca shrieked. 'She's brought tears to your eyes.'

She laughed as he began to rub his arm under his white flannel shirt; but on her cheeks and in her eyes he noticed the effect of the sparkling wine and a kind of controlled craziness that he found far from reassuring.

A few moments later a far away fog-horn bellowed across the pitch-black swell, and one or other among the Shades stopped shuffling, on the games table, the star-incised surfaces of the dominoes.

'Fog at sea. . . .'

'The beam of the Granville lighthouse was sweeping over a sea of cotton-wool a few moments ago,' said another Shade.

But to Philippe the blast of the fog-horn evoked the prolonged blare of a hooting car as it sped away along the coast road, and he leapt to his feet.

'It's coming on again,' Vinca mocked.

Adept at self-concealment, she had turned her back to the Shades, and her gaze followed Philippe like a lamentation.

'Nothing of the sort,' he said. 'But I'm feeling dead tired, so if you'll excuse me, I think I'll go up to bed. Good night, Maman, good night, Father. . . . Good night, Madame Ferret. . . . Good night . . .'

'We'll let you off the rest of your litany to-night, my boy.'

'Would you like a cup of weak camomile tea brought up to you?'

'Don't forget to open your window wide.'

'Vinca, did you take your bottle of salts to Phil's room?'

The friendly voices of the Shades followed him as far as the door, a rather faded tutelary wreath of faint-scented dried herbs. He exchanged with Vinca the customary good-night kiss, which as a rule glanced off her proffered cheek toward the ear, and ended up on her neck or the corner of her downy mouth. Then the door closed behind him, the propitiating garland was severed, and he found himself alone.

His room, agape to the moonless sky, accorded him a cold welcome. Hostile and none too strong, he stood beneath the bulb, bagged in yellow muslin, sniffing the smell Vinca called 'boy's smell': school books, leather case packed and ready for the day after the next, bitumen from rubber-soled shoes, cakes of toilet soap and scented hair oil.

He was not suffering particularly; but he felt exiled and utterly exhausted, for which the best remedy is total oblivion. He hurried into bed, put out the lamp, and snuggled down instinctively into the place against the wall where, during nights of childhood illnesses and the later fevers of youth, he had found better cover and protection when the sheet was amply tucked in, and watched the action of his dreams, affected by the moon, high tides, or July thunderstorms, unfold across the flower-patterned paper. He went to sleep at once, only to be assailed by all the usual bad dreams and others most vividly revolting. In one, Camille Dalleray had Vinca's head and face; in another, a crudely improper Vinca held authoritative sway over him with all the cold aloofness of a magician. But in these dreams, Camille Dalleray and Vinca both refused to remember that Philippe was only a young and tender little boy, who longed for nothing better than to nestle his head against a shoulder – a little boy of ten years old. . . .

He woke to find by his watch that it was only a quarter to twelve, and so he would have to squander the remainder of his feverish night in the midst of a sleeping household; he slipped on his sandals, tied the cord of his bath gown tight round his waist, and went downstairs.

The moon, in the first quarter, was a burnished sickle rising over the top of the cliff. It shed no light over the landscape and appeared to be extinguished at every turn – now red, now green – of the revolving Granville lighthouse. Yet, because of its presence, the clumps of foliage were not totally submerged by the night and the white pebble-dashed walls looked faintly phosphorescent between the projecting wooden beams of the villa. Leaving the french windows open, Philippe stepped out into the mild night as into a melancholy but sure refuge. He sat down on the bare damp-resisting earth of the terrace, crammed with the accumulated refuse of sixteen summer holidays, from which Lisette's spade occasionally exhumed an oxidized fragment of some antique toy that had lain there buried for ten, twelve, or fifteen years. . . .

He felt disconsolate, worldly wise, outside the pale. 'Perhaps it's all part of becoming a man,' he thought. He was worried, and to no purpose, by the unconscious need to find someone to whom he could confide his sadness and his worldly wisdom, like all honest little atheists for whom a secular education provides no all-seeing God.

'Is that you, Phil?'

The voice came down to him like a leaf on the wind. He got up and walked noiselessly across to the window with a wooden balcony.

'Yes,' he breathed. 'Aren't you asleep?'

'Obviously not. I'm coming down.'

Before he had heard a sound, she was standing close beside him. All he had seen of her approach was a whitish face suspended above a silhouette that seemed part and parcel of the night itself.

'Won't you feel cold?'

'No. I've put on my blue kimono. Besides it's mild enough. Don't let's stay here.'

'Why weren't you asleep?'

'I didn't feel sleepy. I was thinking. Don't let's stay here. We shall wake someone up.'

'I don't want to go down to the beach at this time of night, you'll catch cold.'

'I'm not in the habit of catching cold. But it wasn't my idea to go down to the beach, you know. I'd rather go for a short stroll up the hill.'

She spoke in a voice that was hard to catch, yet Philippe never missed a single word. Its toneless quality afforded him infinite pleasure. It was no longer Vinca's voice, or any woman's for that matter, but simply a little presence, almost invisible, with something familiar about it; a little presence, devoid of all bitterness, suggestive of a stroll in the still watches of the night . . .

His foot struck against some object and she put out a hand to steady him.

'It's sure to be the geranium pots, didn't you see them?'

'No.'

'Neither did I. But I can see them as the blind do, I know that they are there. . . . Take care that there isn't a trowel lying somewhere beside them.'

'How do you know that?'

'Oh, just an idea I've got it should be there. And it would make a noise like the clatter of a coal shovel. . . . There, what did I tell you!'

Philippe was entranced by this naughty little whispering. He could have wept with relief and pleasure at finding Vinca so sweet and, among the shadows, just like the Vinca of the old days when she was only twelve and used to whisper in the same way, bending over the wet sand, with the full moon dancing on the bellies of the fish during their midnight netting escapades.

'You remember, Vinca, the time we went fishing at midnight with the big square dipping-net?'

'And you caught bronchitis. That proved a splendid excuse for putting a stop to our fishing at night. . . . Listen! . . . Did you close the french windows?'

'No. . . .'

'The wind's freshening, don't you hear, and they're beginning to rattle? Oh, if I didn't think of everything . . .'

She disappeared and returned like a sylph on feet so light that Phil only guessed her approach from the scent wafted on the wind ahead of her.

'What on earth's that scent you've got on, Vinca? How strong you smell of it!'

'Don't speak so loud. I was feeling so hot that I gave myself a spirit rub before coming down.'

He made no further comment, but now that his attention was awakened he did indeed register that she thought of everything.

'Go on through, Phil. I'm holding the gate open. Try not to tread on the lettuces.'

The proximity of the sea could easily be forgotten among all the market garden aromas that rose from the cultivated soil. Philippe rasped his bare legs on a low wall of dense thyme and in passing let his fingers brush along the velvety muzzles of the snapdragons.

'You know, Vinca, that in the kitchen garden one can't hear a sound that may come from the house, because of this cluster of bushes!'

'But no sound is coming from the house, Phil. And besides, we're doing no harm.'

She had picked up a little windfall pear that had ripened prematurely and smelt of musk from the insect inside it.

He heard her bite into it and then throw it away.

'What are you up to? You're eating something?'

'It's only one of those yellow pears. But it wasn't good enough to let you have it.'

Philippe's vague resentment was not to be broken down altogether by her exceptional lack of restraint. He found Vinca a little too sweet, airy and serene as a sylph, and he suddenly thought of the laughter of nuns and how through its maddening genteel affectedness there rings a mirthless gaiety that might have escaped from the tomb. 'I'd very much like to see her face,' he said to himself. And he shivered to think that the toneless voice and the playful girlish words might have issued from the convulsed mask, its own colours heightened and shining with rage, when confronting his in their nest among the rocks.

'Vinca, listen. Let's go back in.'

'If you wish. Just one moment more. Let me have one moment more. I'm so happy. What about you? We're both so happy. How easy life is at night! But not indoors. Oh, how I've come to loathe my room these last few days. Out here, I have no fears. . . . A glow-worm, look! So late in the season! No, don't try to catch it. . . . Silly, why are you trembling so? It's only a cat out on the prowl. At night they hunt field-mice.'

He caught the sound of a little laugh, and Vinca's arm tightened round his waist. His ear was attuned to the slightest breath, the least snap of a twig, held entranced, despite his uneasiness, by the variety of unceasing whisperings. Far from being frightened of the dark, Vinca threaded her way through it as through a familiar and well-loved landscape, explaining it all to Philippe as she guided him like a blind guest for whom she was performing the midnight honours.

'Vinca darling, let's go back.'

She made a little toad-like croak.

'Oh, you've called me Vinca darling! Why can't it always be night? At this particular moment you're no longer the person who deceived me, and I'm not the person who has suffered so much. Oh, Phil, don't let's go back to the house just yet, let me be a little happy, a little loving, as certain of you as I was in my dreams. Phil . . . Phil, you don't know me.'

'Perhaps I don't, Vinca darling.'

They stumbled over some sort of coarse hay that crackled under their footsteps.

'It's the threshed saracen corn,' Vinca said. 'They were threshing it by flail to-day.'

'How do you know?'

'All the time we were having our heated argument, didn't you hear the thuds of the two flails? I heard them. Sit down, Phil.'

'She . . . she heard them. . . . She was frantic, she struck my face, she never drew breath as the words kept pouring out – yet she heard the thudding of the two flails!'

He could not help comparing this awareness of all her feminine senses with his memory of a certain other feminine skill. . . .

'Don't go away and leave me, Phil! I've not been naughty; I've not cried, I've not scolded. . . .'

Her round head, beneath its evenly-cut silken hair, rolled up and down against his shoulder, and the warmth of her cheek brought warmth to his.

'Kiss me, Phil, please. Please. . . .'

He kissed her, blending with his own pleasure the inept

clumsiness of extreme youth that looks no further than the gratification of its own desires, and the all too precise memory of a kiss that other lips had taken from his, but not for the asking. But pressed to his lips he felt the form and shape of Vinca's mouth, still tasting of the fruit she had just bitten into, felt the haste of her lips to open and discover their secret that they might squander its sweetness on his – and he swayed in the darkness. 'I really believe that we are lost,' he thought. 'Oh, that it may happen quickly, since it must, and since she now could never wish for it to be otherwise. Oh God, how wonderful and inevitable her mouth is, and so understanding since the first time our lips met! Oh, let it happen quickly, quickly. . . . '

But possession is a miracle not so speedily accomplished. His neck was held in a tight embrace by an arm that would not let go its hold. He tried to shake it free, but Vinca only tightened her grip, thinking Philippe must wish to end their kiss. At length he seized the stiffened wrist close to his ear and flung her backwards on to the bed of straw. She gave a little moan and did not move again; but when, half ashamed, he leaned over her body, she caught hold of him again and held him close. There they lay, like brother and sister, enjoying a pleasant interlude, each showing the other a little pity and affection with the circumspection of experienced lovers. On his reversed arm Philippe held an invisible Vinca, and with his free hand he stroked her skin, already aware of its delicacy and of every mark scratched or incised upon it by the prick of a thorn or the sharp point of a rock. She tried to laugh as she begged him in a whisper. 'Do leave my beautiful grazes alone. . . . What do you want with those, when we have this lovely soft straw to lie on. . . . '

But he could hear her breath trembling in her words, and trembled himself. Again and again he returned to her mouth, the one thing about her he knew least of all. He resolved, during a respite for breath, to spring to his feet and make a dash for the house. But as he drew away from Vinca, he was seized with horror at finding his arms empty and the air cold, as if his whole body had been suddenly denuded, and he went back to her body with an impulse she matched, so that their knees became interlaced. Then he summoned up the courage to call her 'Vinca darling' in humble accents, beseeching her to grant him what he asked of her and at the same time to forget what it was he wanted of her. She understood, giving way perhaps to an excessive exasperation at finding no words, and bruising herself in her haste. He heard a brief cry of remonstrance and felt an involuntary contortion, but the body he was handling so roughly neither flinched nor demanded respite.

HE slept little but soundly, and got out of bed convinced that the whole house was empty. But downstairs he saw the caretaker with his non-barking dog and all his fishing gear, and from the first floor came the sound of his father's early morning cough. He went and hid himself between the spindlewood hedge and the terrace wall to spy on Vinca's window. A fresh breeze was chivvying the clouds that melted at its breath; by turning his head he could see the sails of the Cancale fishing smacks cradled on a short steep sea. All the windows of the house were still shuttered.

'What about her, is she still asleep? They're always said to weep, after. Perhaps Vinca is crying now. Yet at this moment she ought to be lying in my arms as we used to lie on the sandy links. Then I should say to her "It isn't true. It never really happened. You're just my Vinca, as you always were. You never gave me that moment of happiness, which didn't amount to so very much, after all. None of it ever occurred, not even your sigh or your song that broke off almost as soon as begun, which made you suddenly grow heavy and stiff as a corpse in my arms. None of it is true. If, this evening, I disappeared along the road to Ker-Anna and to-morrow crept in by myself before dawn, I should manage it so skilfully that you'd never know. . . . Let's go for a walk along the shore and let's take Lisette with us."'

It never occured to him that it might be possible to perfect the give-and-take of an act of pleasure so clumsily performed. He was driven by the idealism of his tender age to salvage only what he knew must not be allowed to perish: his fifteen enchanted years of single-minded affection, their fifteen years together as pure and loving twins.

'I should say to her, "You are wrong if you think that our love, the Phil-and-Vinca love, ends there, there on the bed of threshed saracen corn, prickly with straw. It leads elsewhere than to the bed in your room, or in mine. It only goes to show, believe me! Since the love given me by a woman I never knew is a joy so lasting that it makes me quiver, even when she is far away, like the heart of an eel that goes on quivering after it has been cut from the living body, what do you suppose our love couldn't do to us? It only goes to show. . . . But if I do happen to be wrong, then you must never know that I'm wrong. . . . "

'I should say to her. "It is a dream come true before its time, a delirious dream, a torture you had to endure while biting your hand, you poor brave little pal playing opposite me in my dilemma. For you it was a dream, and perhaps a frightful one; for me the humiliation was worse, an experience less surprising than the introspective delights of solitude. But nothing will be lost, if you can forget all about it, and I myself can expunge the memory of something that was mercifully veiled by the shades of night. . . . No, I never gripped your flexible body between my knees – Now take me on your back, and let's ride-a-cock-horse across the sands. . . . " '

When he heard the jingle of her curtains being drawn, it required all his courage for him not to turn away his head.

Vinca appeared between the flaps of the shutters as she folded them back against the outside wall. She stood blinking her eyes deliberately and staring fixedly in front of her. Then she plunged both her hands into her thick hair and from her tousled head drew out a wisp of straw. Blushing and laughing simultaneously, she leaned forward and peered out from her dishevelled mop, no doubt looking for Philippe himself. Wide awake by now, she fetched from her room behind her a varnished earthenware pitcher, and carefully watered the purple-flowering fuchsia on her wooden balcony. She looked up at the clear blue sky that gave promise of fine weather, and began to sing the little song she sang every morning. Hidden among the spindlewood, Philippe kept watch, like a man who had come there to make an attempt on her life.

'She's singing. . . . I suppose I must believe my eyes and ears, she's actually singing. And she's just watered the fuchsia.'

It never for an instant crossed his mind that such an apparition ought to bring joy to his heart, so exactly did it fit the recent vows he had made to himself. He stopped short only at the thought that he might be deceiving himself, and, too young and inexperienced for self-analysis, he pig-headedly started to draw a comparison.

'I came here one night, under this window, to knock my brains out, because, in a revealing flash, a thunderbolt had just fallen between my childhood and the present. And here she is singing . . . singing. . . . '

Vinca's eyes vied with the bright blue of the morning sea. She was combing her hair, and once again started to sing through pursed lips, over which played a vague smile.

'She's singing. She'll look lovely at breakfast. She'll shout "Lisette, pinch him till it hurts!" No great good and no great harm will have come of it, I dare say, for there she stands unaffected. . . . '

He saw that Vinca was leaning out over the balcony crushing her breasts against the wooden support, gazing in the direction of his room.

'If only I could appear at the window opposite and leap across the balcony to join her, she would throw her arms round my neck. . . .

'O you that I call "my master", why did you sometimes seem to me to be more miraculous than this little novice with all her simple ways! You went away without telling me the whole story. If it was only the pride of those who derive their pleasure from giving that made you care for me, then to-day, for the first time, you should take pity on me. . . .'

From the window came a faint, happy little tune that passed over his head. Nor did the thought strike him that in a few weeks' time the child who was singing might well be standing in tears, doomed and frantic, at the same window. He hid his face in the hollow of the arm on which he was leaning and pondered his own insignificance, his downfall, his kindliness. 'Neither a hero, nor yet an executioner. . . . A little pain, a little pleasure. . . . That's all I shall have given her, that and nothing else . . . nothing . . .'

FOR THE BEST IN PAPERBACKS, LOOK FOR THE

In every corner of the world, on every subject under the sun, Penguin represents quality and variety – the very best in publishing today.

For complete information about books available from Penguin – including Pelicans, Puffins, Peregrines and Penguin Classics – and how to order them, write to us at the appropriate address below. Please note that for copyright reasons the selection of books varies from country to country.

In the United Kingdom: For a complete list of books available from Penguin in the U.K., please write to *Dept E.P., Penguin Books Ltd, Harmondsworth, Middlesex, UB7 0DA*

In the United States: For a complete list of books available from Penguin in the U.S., please write to *Dept BA, Penguin, 299 Murray Hill Parkway, East Rutherford, New Jersey 07073*

In Canada: For a complete list of books available from Penguin in Canada, please write to *Penguin Books Canada Ltd, 2801 John Street, Markham, Ontario L3R 1B4*

In Australia: For a complete list of books available from Penguin in Australia, please write to the *Marketing Department, Penguin Books Australia Ltd, P.O. Box 257, Ringwood, Victoria 3134*

In New Zealand: For a complete list of books available from Penguin in New Zealand, please write to the *Marketing Department, Penguin Books (NZ) Ltd, Private Bag, Takapuna, Auckland 9*

In India: For a complete list of books available from Penguin, please write to *Penguin Overseas Ltd, 706 Eros Apartments, 56 Nehru Place, New Delhi, 110019*

In Holland: For a complete list of books available from Penguin in Holland, please write to *Penguin Books Nederland B.V., Postbus 195, NL–1380AD Weesp, Netherlands*

In Germany: For a complete list of books available from Penguin, please write to *Penguin Books Ltd, Friedrichstrasse 10 – 12, D–6000 Frankfurt Main 1, Federal Republic of Germany*

In Spain: For a complete list of books available from Penguin in Spain, please write to *Longman Penguin España, Calle San Nicolas 15, E–28013 Madrid, Spain*

FOR THE BEST IN PAPERBACKS, LOOK FOR THE 🐧

PENGUIN MODERN CLASSICS

Death of a Salesman Arthur Miller

One of the great American plays of the century, this classic study of failure brings to life an unforgettable character: Willy Loman, the shifting and inarticulate hero who is nonetheless a unique individual.

The Echoing Grove Rosamund Lehmann

'No English writer has told of the pains of women in love more truly or more movingly than Rosamund Lehmann' – Marghenita Laski. 'This novel is one of the most absorbing I have read for years' – Simon Raven, *Listener*

Pale Fire Vladimir Nabokov

This book contains the last poem by John Shade, together with a Preface, notes and Index by his posthumous editor. But is the eccentric editor more than just haughty and intolerant – mad, bad, perhaps even dangerous . . .?

The Man Who Was Thursday G. K. Chesterton

This hilarious extravaganza concerns a secret society of revolutionaries sworn to destroy the world. But when Thursday turns out to be not a poet but a Scotland Yard detective, one starts to wonder about the identity of the others . . .

The Rebel Albert Camus

Camus's attempt to understand 'the time I live in' tries to justify innocence in an age of atrocity. 'One of the vital works of our time, compassionate and disillusioned, intelligent but instructed by deeply felt experience' – *Observer*

Letters to Milena Franz Kafka

Perhaps the greatest collection of love letters written in the twentieth century, they are an orgy of bliss and despair, of ecstasy and desperation poured out by Kafka in his brief two-year relationship with Milena Jesenska.

FOR THE BEST IN PAPERBACKS, LOOK FOR THE

PENGUIN MODERN CLASSICS

The Age of Reason   Jean-Paul Sartre

The first part of Sartre's classic trilogy, set in the volatile Paris summer of 1938, is itself 'a dynamic, deeply disturbing novel' (Elizabeth Bowen) which tackles some of the major issues of our time.

Three Lives   Gertrude Stein

A turning point in American literature, these portraits of three women – thin, worn Anna, patient, gentle Lena and the complicated, intelligent Melanctha – represented in 1909 one of the pioneering examples of modernist writing.

Doctor Faustus   Thomas Mann

Perhaps the most convincing description of an artistic genius ever written, this portrait of the composer Leverkuhn is a classic statement of one of Mann's obsessive themes: the discord between genius and sanity.

The New Machiavelli   H. G. Wells

This autobiography of a man who has thrown up a glittering political career and marriage to go into exile with the woman he loves also contains an illuminating Introduction by Melvyn Bragg.

The Collected Poems of Stevie Smith

Amused, amusing and deliciously barbed, this volume includes many poems which dwell on death; as a whole, though, as this first complete edition in paperback makes clear, Smith's poetry affirms an irrepressible love of life.

Rhinoceros / The Chairs / The Lesson   Eugène Ionesco

Three great plays by the man who was one of the founders of what has come to be known as the Theatre of the Absurd.

FOR THE BEST IN PAPERBACKS, LOOK FOR THE

PENGUIN MODERN CLASSICS

The Second Sex   Simone de Beauvoir

This great study of Woman is a landmark in feminist history, drawing together insights from biology, history and sociology as well as literature, psychoanalysis and mythology to produce one of the supreme classics of the twentieth century.

The Bridge of San Luis Rey   Thornton Wilder

On 20 July 1714 the finest bridge in all Peru collapsed, killing 5 people. Why? Did it reveal a latent pattern in human life? In this beautiful, vivid and compassionate investigation, Wilder asks some searching questions in telling the story of the survivors.

Parents and Children   Ivy Compton-Burnett

This richly entertaining introduction to the world of a unique novelist brings to light the deadly claustrophobia within a late-Victorian upper-middle-class family . . .

Vienna 1900   Arthur Schnitzler

These deceptively languid sketches, four 'games with love and death', lay bare an astonishing and disturbing world of sexual turmoil (which anticipates Freud's discoveries) beneath the smooth surface of manners and convention.

Confessions of Zeno   Italo Svevo

Zeno, an innocent in a corrupt world, triumphs in the end through his stoic acceptance of his own failings in this extraordinary, experimental novel which fuses memory, obsession and desire.

The House of Mirth   Edith Wharton

Lily Bart – beautiful, intelligent and charming – is trapped like a butterfly in the inverted jam jar of wealthy New York society . . . This tragic comedy of manners was one of Wharton's most shocking and innovative books.

BY THE SAME AUTHOR

'I know of few works which have today offered me such an amused and perfect joy' – *Andre Gide*

'There is nothing to explain, nothing to criticize, one has only to admire' – *Henri de Montherlant*

'A versatile and subtle original of undeniably high quality' – *Martin Seymour Smith*

CAPTIVE
CHANCE ACQUAINTANCES *and* JULIE DE CARNEILHAN
CLAUDINE AT SCHOOL
CLAUDINE IN PARIS
CLAUDINE MARRIED
CLAUDINE AND ANNIE
CHERI *and* THE LAST OF CHERI
COLLECTED STORIES
GIGI *and* THE CAT
INNOCENT LIBERTINE
MY MOTHER'S HOUSE *and* SIDO
PURE AND THE IMPURE
VAGABOND